DEAD RECKONING

"Dusty," Doc Leroy said, crossing to the table and looking, if possible, even more pallid and studious than usual, "you know that feller Lon had to shoot last night."

"I'm not likely to forget *him* any too soon," the small Texan replied.

"I thought there was something strange about him when you brought him in and told us what happened," Doc continued. "So I've been down to the undertaker's and took a closer look. You'll *never* guess what I found out."

"Which being the case, there's not a whole heap of point in us trying," the Ysabel Kid put in, realizing that only something exceptionally out of the ordinary could have produced such a show of emotion from the slender cowhand. "So why not just tell us?"

"That's what I'm aiming to, given the chance," Doc answered. "You-all shot him through the head *last night*—but he's been dead for at least a month."

THE NIGHTHAWK

J.T. EDSON

A DELL BOOK

Published by
Dell Publishing
a division of
Bantam Doubleday Dell
Publishing Group, Inc.
666 Fifth Avenue
New York, New York 10103

This book was originally published in Great Britain under the title SET A-FOOT by Corgi Books, a division of Transworld Publishers, Ltd.

ISBN: 0-440-20726-6

Printed in the United States of America

August 1990

10 9 8 7 6 5 4 3 2 1

RAD

AUTHOR'S NOTE

Reader's who have studied the list of titles in chronological order will notice that this episode in the Floating Outfit series is no longer in the position which it used to occupy. This has come about due to the investigations I have made during my two visits to Fort Worth, Texas. My examination of various documents supplied by members of the Hardin, Fog, and Blaze Clan with whom I consulted showed me that I had been in error and the events recorded hereafter occurred much earlier in Waco's association with Dusty Fog than I had previously envisaged.

J. T. Edson
Active Member, Western Writers of America
Melton Mowbray, England

For Penelope Wallace
with thanks for letting me publish
CAP FOG, TEXAS RANGER,
MEET MR. J. G. REEDER

CHAPTER ONE

IT WOULDN'T'VE HURT *HIM!*

"Well, we-all've found the Rio Grande, I reckon, Lem," the young Negro who answered to the name "Tarbrush" remarked as, having quenched his own thirst, he stood waiting for his big brown mule to finish drinking. "Only thing now is, which way do we head for Bannock's Ford?"

Close to six foot in height, with a lanky yet wiry frame, Tarbrush had a good-looking face, which usually had a cheerful expression. His garments—a low-crowned, wide-brimmed gray J. B. Stetson hat, black wolfskin jacket, dark blue shirt, Levi's pants with the legs outside sharp-toed, high-heeled boots—were indications that he was employed in the cattle industry, which was chiefly responsible for a return to economic stability in Texas after the financial distress caused by having supported the Confederate States in the War of Secession.* There was a Ballard single-shot cartridge carbine in the boot attached to the left side of his low-horned, double-girthed† range saddle and he had an old Colt 1851 Navy revolver tucked through his trouser's waist-

* How this came about is told in GOODNIGHT'S DREAM (American title: THE FLOATING OUTFIT) and FROM HIDE AND HORN.—J.T.E.

† Because of the word "cinch" having Spanish and Mexican connotations, the majority of Texans employ the term "girth"—generally pronounced "girt"—for the broad, short band made from coarsely woven horsehair, canvas, or cordage and terminating at each end with a metal ring which, together with the latigo, is used to fasten a saddle upon a mount's back. As Texans fastened the end of the lariat to the saddlehorn when roping, instead of employing a dally which could be slipped free in an emergency, their rigs had two girths for greater security—J.T.E.

1

band. As he was traveling in search of work, he was carrying the rest of his worldly goods in the bedroll strapped to his rig's cantle.

There was good cause for Tarbrush's comment. Hitherto his life had been spent farther north in Texas, and he was paying his first visit to the border country. While the three-quarter moon gave sufficient illumination for him to be able to look across the Rio Grande to the Mexican shore, there was thick woodland on either side of him. This, together with a bend in the river, prevented him from seeing even a glow of lights to suggest whether his destination lay up- or downstream of his present position. Nor was he close enough to hear anything that might have served as a clue.

Mounting the mule, the young Negro rode back toward the trail that ran parallel to the river. Hearing the sound of hooves as he was emerging from the bushes, he glanced around. In spite of the trees that fringed it there was enough light for him to have a clear view along the trail. As yet the riders were not in sight. Bringing his mule to a halt he waited to ask for directions and hoped that he might have company on the rest of the journey. What he observed a few seconds later suggested that the latter might prove undesirable, or even dangerous, if it materialized.

Spread in a line across the trail the three riders who appeared were behaving in a manner that was calculated to disturb a solitary Negro traveling at night through thick woodland and far from the nearest human habitation. While the worst abuses of the Reconstruction period had been brought to an end, the animosities they had created were not forgotten. There were men, black and white, who would take every opportunity to exercise their hatred of the other race.

Born and raised in the Texas range country, reasonably skilled at handling the revolver and the carbine, Tarbrush was neither a coward nor a reckless hothead. So, although the trio displayed surprise at seeing him, he was careful to avoid making any gesture that might be construed as attempting to reach for either weapon. Instead, he continued to lounge on the motionless mule's saddle and kept his hands in plain sight. For all that, he was ready to take any action that became necessary as he watched them riding closer.

Nursing a Winchester Model of 1866 rifle across his knees, the man on the left was tall, well built, and of early middle age. There was a controlled hardness about his rugged features that was apparent even in the moonlight, and his neatly trimmed black moustache did nothing to soften it. He had on range-style clothing of exceptionally good quality, the dark green shirt and matching bandana having a glossy texture suggestive of silk, with an ivory-handled Colt 1860 Army revolver in a fast-draw holster tied to his right thigh. Sitting a powerful bay gelding he had neither a bedroll nor a rope attached to his saddle. Of the three he had shown the least reaction to discovering Tarbrush in front of them. After a quick glance he had given his attention to scanning the woodland between the trail and the river.

Almost as tall, the rider on the right of the trio was several years younger and slimmer. Good looking, there was a sullen truculence to the lines of his face. He was somewhat more flashily dressed, although in a similar cowhand fashion, and his gun belt supported a brace of Army Colts. At the sight of Tarbrush he had made as if to raise the Henry rifle that was cradled across the crook of his left arm and refrained when the man on the left made a low-spoken, but clearly prohibitive, comment. However, he continued to watch the young Negro.

To Tarbrush's range-wise scrutiny the outer riders' appearance suggested that they probably earned their living through skill with their weapons rather than by ability as cowhands, and unless he was mistaken, the older was much the more capable. He also deduced, from the way in which they were carrying their rifles exposed, that they might be doing something more than merely heading for the town of Bannock's Ford in search of harmless recreation.

While the flanking pair were dressed in a manner that could have passed without arousing too much speculation in most places west of the Big Muddy,* where well-armed men were the exception rather than the rule, the same did not apply to their companion. He might be displaying an equal competence at sitting a Texas-style saddle and handling a horse, but there the resemblance ended.

Stocky of build and medium in height, the third man's clean-shaven face had the slightly Oriental cast of a Mid-European. Unlike the other two he showed no sign of being armed. In fact, his attire was more suited to the streets of an eastern city than for wearing on a trail in the border country of Texas. His round-topped brown hat had a small and curly brim that would offer no protection from the elements. Nor was his short black jacket, white shirt, dark silk cravat, tight-legged tan riding breeches, and Hessian boots† any more appropriate raiment for such terrain. He, too, continued to gaze at Tarbrush.

"Do you-all reckon he saw it in there, Silkie?" asked the youngest of the three horsemen, either unaware or not caring that the dense nature of the woodland on each side of the trail created an acoustic effect that allowed Tarbrush as well as his companions to hear what he was saying.

"No," replied the rider on the right, also apparently failing to appreciate that his words were carrying to the subject of his companion's question. "If he had, he wouldn't be sitting there like nothing had happened."

"Hell!" protested the first speaker. "He's black. It wouldn't've hurt *him!*"

"He wouldn't've known *that,* nor stayed around for long enough to find out, happen he'd seen it coming his way," declared the other man who was wearing range country clothing. He continued his scrutiny of the trees and bushes

---

* Big Muddy, colloquial name for the Mississippi River.—J.T.E.
† Hessian boots: footwear originally designed for use by light cavalry such as Hussars, the knee-length legs having a V-shaped notch in front.—J.T.E.

alongside the trail. "He'd've taken one look and took off like his butt was on fire."

"Hell, yes, he would," the youngest man conceded and, clearly struck by a thought, swung his head toward the one who had not yet spoken. Hefting his rifle, as if wishing to make certain that there was nothing to impede him in raising the butt speedily to his shoulder, he went on, "Are you-all *sure* you can handle that blasted thing, happen we find it, Mr. Petrov? We don't have our faces bla—"

"Of course I can handle it!" interrupted the third member of the party, turning his gaze to the speaker. His voice was harsh and held a different kind of accent from the other two's southern drawls, so that the words emerged as "Hoff gorse I gan handle it" and suggested English was not his native tongue. Having answered, he looked in the other direction and continued, "What do you think he's doing here, Mr. Roelich?"

"I was wondering about that myself," the older of the westerners admitted.

"Quickest way to find out'd be to ask him," the youngster commented, eyeing Tarbrush with a mixture of truculence and disdain.

"Likely, *Mr.* Hooper, but leave *me* to do the asking," the other range-clad man said, and politely as they were spoken, the words came out as an order to an inferior rather than a request. Bringing his horse to a halt he addressed the young Negro in exactly the same tone. "Howdy."

"Howdy, gents," Tarbrush replied, forcing himself to sound amiable despite a growing feeling of trepidation, as the second and third riders caused their mounts to step alongside the first's and not more than fifteen feet away. He decided that something more than the bare greeting was called for and considered an explanation of his presence might not come amiss. "Be right obliged happen you-all can tell me how I can get to Bannock's Ford."

"It's maybe three miles down this way," stated the man who had appointed himself spokesman for the trio, nodding in the direction that they had been riding. His gaze went to the mule, studying its legs in particular, then lifted to its rider's face. "You-all just come over from Mexico?"

"Nope," Tarbrush answered, knowing that his mount showed no signs to suggest it had crossed the river and realizing what was wanted from him. "Feller I asked up to Cotulla allowed I should head straight south to reach Bannock's. When I saw the water through the trees, I figured ole Lem here 'n' me'd take us a drink and make sure we'd hit the Rio Grande, then see if there was anything to show us which way to go from here."

"What brought you-all down he—?" the youngest member of the trio commenced, having been listening with ill-concealed impatience, but the words faded off as his companions glared at him.

"Don't pay him no never-mind," the older westerner drawled, returning his gaze to Tarbrush. For all the comment he continued with what he clearly knew to be an intrusion upon the Negro's private affairs. "Would you be going to Bannock's to visit with your kinfolk?"

"Don't have any there," Tarbrush corrected, sensing the question was a trap. "I'm looking for work. From what I've heard, I ought to be able to get took on as a Nighthawk* easy enough around town."

"You ought," the spokesman admitted, flickering a coldly prohibitive glance as "Mr. Hooper" moved restlessly on his saddle and seemed on the point of injecting a comment. "Only, I'd've thought there'd be plenty of places farther north where you could've got taken on without needing to come down here."

"Sure there were," Tarbrush conceded, so blandly that he managed to conceal his ever-growing resentment. "Trouble being that all them fellers I talked to up there're trailing

---

* Nighthawk: a man hired to look after the horses in the remuda while the rest of a trail drive or roundup crew, except the hands riding night herd on the cattle, were asleep.—J.T.E.

6

herds to Kansas. I've done that twice already and want to try someplace different."

Although the young Negro considered that being subjected to such an interrogation was an unwarrantable liberty, he also appreciated that in the circumstances it would be inadvisable for him to disclose his sentiments. From the names mentioned by Hooper and the easterner, added to what he remembered having heard in the past, he felt sure that he could identify the man who was doing most of the talking. The knowledge was an effective curb against raising a protest.

When men noted for speed on the draw were being discussed, Lawrence Rudolph Roelich—whose sobriquet "Silkie" had arisen from his predilection for wearing shirts and even, it was rumored, socks of that material—would not have been among the first to be considered. For all that, he was still regarded as being a *pistolero valiente* of better than average ability. Unlike the younger hardcase he was displaying neither arrogance nor truculence. His questions were being delivered in an almost matter-of-fact tone, but his demeanor warned Tarbrush that he had every intention of having them answered. What was more, even if he had been alone, he possessed sufficient skill in the use of firearms to enforce his desire for information if it should not be supplied voluntarily.

Distasteful as having to submit to the questioning might be, there was a second factor compelling Tarbrush to do so. All through the conversation the man in the Eastern-style garments had never stopped looking at him and he was finding the unwinking scrutiny becoming increasingly disconcerting. Only once before, when as a child he had been taken to have his "future" foretold by an old conjure-woman who was reputed to possess mystical and supernatural powers, had he encountered anything to match the piercing intensity of the dark, somewhat slanting eyes. They gave him the feeling that they could probe into his thoughts and would know whether or not he was speaking the truth. It was an eerie and far from comforting sensation.

At the conclusion of Tarbrush's explanation regarding his presence in the area, the easterner addressed him for the first time. However, as the words were not in English, he could not understand what they meant.

"I'm sorry, mister," the young Negro said, hoping that the perturbation he was experiencing did not show. "I can't make out what you're saying."

Speaking again, the man either repeated his words or made some equally unintelligible comment. On receiving the same negative response from Tarbrush, he looked in an interrogative manner at Roelich. The *pistolero* gave what was clearly a nod of confirmation to the unasked question. Apparently the man was satisfied by his companion's summation. Instead of reverting to English he rose on his stirrups and peered at the woodland to the left of the trail.

"You shouldn't have any trouble getting took on," Roelich drawled. "I've heard there's at least two trail crews in town. You can ride along with us if you've a mind."

While Tarbrush felt relieved at the harsh-voiced foreigner's eyes having left him, he was less pleased with the *pistolero*'s proposition. A shrewd judge of character and always susceptible to atmosphere, he had started to consider that the former could prove to be the most dangerous member of the trio. He had had sufficient experience with men like the two hardcases to know how to cope with, or at least avoid antagonizing, them. However, their companion was something far beyond his ken. For some reason he could not entirely understand, his every instinct gave a warning that the man in the eastern clothes was a person to be avoided. The feeling was so strong that he could not bring himself to remain in the other's company.

"Ole Lem here's done a fair piece of traveling already today and I figured to let him rest up a spell afore we go any farther," Tarbrush replied, noticing that the easterner darted a glance at Roelich as if he, too, did not favor the suggestion. "Fact being, I only come out when I heard you-all to ask you the way."

"If we say you're coming—!" Hooper began aggressively, but once again fell silent as the older *pistolero* scowled at him.

"That mule sure looks like it's traveled some miles," Roelich told Tarbrush. "And we're wanting to get into Bannock's as quick as we can. Only, was I you, I wouldn't go resting down by the river. It could be mighty dangerous."

"I've got me some protection," the young Negro pointed out, feeling that he should deliver a warning that he was armed and dispel any notions that had been formed with regard to his courage.

"An old *Navy* Colt* and what I'd say is a Ballard one-shooter?" Roelich countered, giving the young Negro's weapons an experienced glance. Pausing to let the implications of his comment be appreciated, he went on, "I've never been one for telling folks what to do, but there's been a whole mess of real bad trouble with a bear down this way recently. Not just a black nor a cinnamon neither, but a full-growed old flatheaded grizzly."

"I've heard tell of such critters," Tarbrush admitted. "And from all accounts they're a whole heap meaner'n any old black or cinnamon bear."†

"This one is, for sure," Roelich warned. "He's taken to

* Used in this context the term *Navy* refers to the caliber; .36 of an inch. Although the military sometimes claimed derisively that it was harder to kill a soldier than a sailor, the weight of the weapon was the deciding factor in the naval authorities' rejection of the .44 "Army" caliber. The revolver they needed would be carried on a seaman's belt and not, handguns having originally and primarily been developed for use by members of the cavalry, by a man who would generally be riding on a horse—J.T.E.

† The large and wholly black "Florida" or "Everglades," small and pure white "Kermode"—found only on the offshore islands and coastal regions of Canada's British Columbia—medium-sized blue-gray "Glacier" or "blue" inhabitant of Alaska's St. Elias Alps, and the reddish- or yellowish-brown "cinnamon" varieties, originally granted the status of subspecies, are now considered to be merely regional color phases of the American black bear, *Euarctos americanus.* None of them were as potentially dangerous and aggressive as the subspecies of *Ursus horribilis,* the grizzly bear.—J.T.E.

attacking and eating folks, which's why we're toting our rifles ready to be used. Like I said, you do what you want. But was it me, I wouldn't stick around too long anywhere close to the river, and was I to hear that old grizzly coming, I'd light out as fast as I could go even though I'm toting a repeater and not a single-shot."

"I take it right kindly for the warning," Tarbrush answered.

"Wouldn't have felt right if I hadn't given it," Roelich replied. "I've seen what that old grizzly's done to them's he's jumped, and believe me, your old Ballard and Navy Colt wouldn't come close to stopping him doing it to you."

"I don't aim on counting on 'em to do it," the young Negro stated and, wondering if the *pistolero* was merely trying to dissuade him from lingering in the vicinity of the river, went on with what he hoped would be an assurance of his intentions. "We've took us a drink already. So we'll just rest up here for a while and, happen we see or hear anything of that old grizzly bear, I'm betting that, tired or not, Lem can run fast enough to get us away from him."

"I reckon he could, unless you left it too late," Roelich conceded and, setting his horse into motion, concluded, "Adios, then. Could be we'll see you-all in Bannock's later on."

"Could be," Tarbrush agreed formally. "Adios."

"What do you make of him, Mr. Roelich?" inquired the man who Hooper had called "Mr. Petrov," after the trio had ridden a short way, and once again, the acoustics caused the words to be carried to the young Negro. "When I told him in French to look around because something was coming, he didn't show any sign of knowing what I meant. But he might have been—how do you say it?—bluffing."

"I don't reckon he was," the older of the westerners declared with complete conviction. "He speaks English without any trace of an accent and it's not likely a nigger from Haiti would know enough about the cattle business to make out he was looking for work as a Nighthawk."

"Then why didn't he ride into the town with us?" Petrov wanted to know.

"Could be he didn't like the look of us. He for sure wasn't too taken with you," Roelich replied. "Or maybe he just doesn't care for white men's company. Some of 'em don't."

"Hey, Silkie," Hooper put in. "Happen Mr. Petrov's worried about that coon, we could easy enough make him come with us."

"We could huh?" Roelich grunted.

"Why not?" Hooper demanded, and raised his rifle a trifle. "I don't see nothing hard about doing it."

"Everything's easy enough, happen you don't look no farther than the muzzle of a gun," Roelich drawled, favoring the young hardcase with a sardonic glance.

"*You* asked him to ride with us!" Hooper protested, nettled by the other man's response.

"Only because I figured he wouldn't, and didn't want him to reckon we wasn't needing his company," Roelich answered.

"Damn it all!" Hooper yelped. "We know's somebody's been sneaking around—"

"There's nothing to suggest it was him," Roelich interrupted. "You likely didn't look, but I did, and he's got bigger feet than whoever made the sign we found."

"They could be in cahoots," Hooper pointed out sullenly.

"They *could,* but he could just's easy've told us the truth," Roelich countered. "And *I* reckon that's more likely. Which being the case, there's no sense in making him think something's wrong. After what I told him about the grizzly, he's not going to wait around should he hear it coming. But have *you-all* thought what it would mean was he along with us and we come across that damned thing?"

"I don't see's how we'd have a whole heap to raise sweat over if we did," Hooper protested, being the kind of person who hated to have his suggestions discarded. "Mr. Petrov allows he can keep it peaceable."

"And what about *him* seeing it?" Roelich asked, giving a jerk of his head in a rearward direction.

"Shucks," Hooper replied, with the air of one who was stating the obvious. "If that happens, we can easy enough drop him in the river and make sure he can't go talking out of turn."

CHAPTER TWO

HE WAS ASKING ABOUT HIRED GUNS

Prosperity, as was the case throughout almost all of Texas, had been brought to Bannock's Ford by the development of the cattle business. Situated at a point where the Rio Grande, having widened, was shallow for much of the year and flowed over an even, firm bottom, the region had always been recognized as offering an easy place at which to cross. However, over the past couple of years, an increased source of revenue had produced an expansion until what was formerly a hamlet of a score or so buildings had blossomed—although there were those who would have protested against the use of such a pleasant description—into a fair-sized town.

The laws of supply and demand were responsible for the change that had come over Bannock's Ford. In addition to producing beef with which to help feed the Indians on reservations and delivering large herds to the railroad towns of Kansas for shipment to meat-hungry eastern states, some of the Texas ranchers had already commenced the migrations that would eventually establish their form of business in every part of the West where it could be carried out. So many cattle had been moved, it was becoming apparent that, greatly as the numbers of the free-ranging animals had multiplied during the War between the States—when most ranching activities had been at a standstill—the demands being made upon them would finally exceed their capacity to reproduce sufficient replacements. What was more, the operators of the hide and tallow factories had been compelled to seek out a cheaper source of supply than was now available in Texas.*

Mexico had offered a solution to the problem. Below the border, where the longhorn cattle were able to breed just as successfully, the owners of ranchos and haciendas lacked a large-scale and lucrative market. Such attempts as had been made to drive herds to Kansas had been rebuffed by the Texans. Not that many had been tried. After contemplating the difficulties the majority of the Mexican landowners had preferred the less hazardous method of selling their surplus stock to their neighbors north of the Rio Bravo,† who in turn would be left with the problems of further disposal.

Because of the advantages offered by the shallows Bannock's Ford had developed into a major point at which the northbound cattle could cross. As was always the case the influx of potential wealth had attracted people who wished to share in—or benefit from—it. No fewer than five saloons now competed for trade along what had become the main street. There were also two hotels, four rooming houses, and a variety of other business enterprises available to cater for the needs of the Texan or Mexican cattlemen, the buyers from the hide and tallow factories who gathered to conduct their affairs, and the cowhands drawn there in search of employment with trail drives. As further evidence of the new affluence the Overland Stage Line created a frequent schedule of its vehicles and set up an office complete with telegraph facilities. In addition captains Miffin Kennedy and Richard King—who combined ranching with operating steamboats along the Rio Grande—found that it paid for their shallow-draft vessels to make the town a regular port of call.

* Providing the only large scale source of disposal for the ranchers in Texas prior to the development of markets based on the railroad towns of Kansas, the hide and tallow factories had been able to purchase vast numbers of cattle for no more than four dollars a head, frequently with calves thrown in free.—J.T.E.

† Rio Bravo: the Mexicans' name for the Rio Grande.—J.T.E.

Riding alone along the busy main street Silkie Roelich could not be numbered among those who regarded the town's mushroomlike growth as advantageous. The way in which the population tended to fluctuate did nothing to make his work easier. Before the traffic in Mexican cattle had produced such popularity, any visitor who had elected to remain in the vicinity would have been sufficient of a novelty to arouse comment. Now, with so many people coming and taking up residence for indefinite periods, the person who apparently was showing such an undesirable interest in his employer's affairs was able to pass unnoticed.

Studying such of the buildings on either side of the street as were still open, Roelich found that luck was with him. The man he had come to consult with was just emerging—slouching out would have been a more apt description—from the well-lit and rowdy interior of the Rio Grande Saloon. He turned away without looking in Roelich's direction. However, despite the lumbering gait, Roelich was pleased to notice that the other showed no sign of being under the influence of liquor. At least, not sufficiently to impair his usefulness.

"Marshal Gormley!" Roelich called, urging his horse to move a little faster.

Hearing his name the man on the saloon's already warped wooden front porch swung ponderously around. Nearly six feet in height, Arthur Gormley had a bulky body that was running to fat and surly porcine features that always seemed in need of a shave. He was wearing a wide-brimmed black hat perched on the back of a close-cropped head of dark hair. His white shirt had no collar and the trousers of his rumpled brown suit were thrust into flat-heeled, mud-smeared riding boots. Partially concealed by the left lapel of his jacket a shield-shaped town marshal's badge of office was pinned to his vest. There was a sawed-off ten-gauge shotgun tucked under his right arm, and around his bulging paunch, a gun belt carried a Colt 1860 Army revolver in a high cavalry-twist holster.

"Howdy, Silkie," Gormley greeted, stepping from the porch. "I wasn't expecting to see you in town tonight. If you're going along to the Man on the Wall—"

"I'm not!" Roelich interrupted, having no liking for the peace officer and drawing a wrong conclusion from his final words. Stopping his horse and swinging down he went on as the other joined him, "We've got some trouble. One of those damned things of the professor's has busted loose and took off."

"The hell you say!" Gormley exclaimed, so alarmed by the news that it swamped his resentment at the blunt rebuffal. He started to move the shotgun into a position of greater readiness.

"Hold your voice down!" Roelich ordered, savagely sotto voce, deciding that the marshal was responding as he had expected and glancing around to make sure nobody was near enough to overhear them.

"Is it headed for town?" Gormley asked, speaking more quietly, having misinterpreted his visitor's actions.

"We don't know which way it's gone," Roelich admitted, relieved to notice that none of the few people on the street were paying any attention to them. "There was no sign of it on the way in, but I've left Petrov and Hooper back at the edge of the woods so they can stop it if it shows up."

"Can they do it?" the marshal demanded, still registering consternation.

"Petrov's always been able to and he allows he can now, without shooting," Roelich replied. "But I thought I'd come in and let you know what's happening in case he can't—"

"I'll go and pass word for my deputies—!" Gormley commenced.

"The hell you will!" Roelich snapped. "Happen it comes to shooting, we don't want *anybody* to see that thing, alive or dead."

"Yeah, but—" Gormley muttered, still looking around uneasily.

"There's near half a mile of clear and flat country between

here and the woods," Roelich pointed out, with what patience he could muster. "And that damned thing's too big to come across without Petrov and Hooper seeing it. All I want from you, if they have to shoot it, is that you make sure *nobody* goes out there to find out what's happening. At least, not until they've had time to hide it."

"That shouldn't be too hard—shots aren't so unusual hereabouts's folks'd take notice of one or two beyond the town limits," Gormley stated, overlooking one possible exception in his eagerness to pass on the information that he had been prevented from giving at the start of the conversation. "Are you staying on here, or going back to Petrov?"

"Going back," Roelich replied. "But, seeing's we'll be waiting out there until morning unless it shows up sooner, I said I'd take a bottle of whiskey and some food for us."

"There's a feller down to the Man on the Wall Saloon's you should take a look at," Gormley explained, although he wished that the hardcase was staying longer in case Petrov and Hooper should fail in their assignment, and the thing (he could think of no other way to describe it) reached the town. "Come in around noon today. From what I've been told, he was asking about hired guns. If there was any of 'em hereabouts and such."

"What's he look like?" Roelich demanded, realizing that he might have misunderstood the peace officer's earlier comment regarding his destination and it had not been made purely for the purpose of soliciting an invitation to be his guest.

"Tall, skinny young cuss wearing a white-handled Army Colt low-tied in a good rig," Gormley answered. "He talks Texan and's dressed like a cowhand, but with that pasty face of his'n, I don't reckon he is one. He's just dressed up so folks'll think he is."

"I'd best go and take a look at him," Roelich decided. "Although, if he's only showed up today, he's not likely to be the one who's been hanging around out by the island."

"Should I come with you?"

"Nope. There's no sense in letting it be too obvious that you're on the professor's payroll."

With that, ignoring Gormley's scowl at the reference to one of the ways in which he augmented his official salary, Roelich turned toward the horse. On the point of mounting he became aware that a figure was standing in the darkness of an alley at the opposite side of the street. As if realizing that it had been observed, the shape moved. Advancing instead of withdrawing into the blackness, it took the form of a slender woman who turned to stroll along the sidewalk.

The light from the window of the general store she was passing showed the woman to be a young and beautiful redhead about five feet seven inches tall. While slim, she was anything but skinny and filled a well-cut dark two-piece traveling costume in an attractive, if not blatantly eye-catching, fashion. Her movements, though graceful, had none of the characteristics that might have suggested a reason for her presence in the alley. Nor did the parasol and vanity bag in her hands supply any clue. Such things were carried by respectable ladies as well as prostitutes in search of customers.

"Who's that?" Roelich asked, as the woman walked onward without as much as a glance in his direction. He knew that his companion would have taken the trouble to learn the identity of such an attractive person.

"Name's Elvira Porterham," the marshal supplied, in tones of disinterest that were informative to anybody who knew him as well as the man he was addressing. "She came in about a week back. Allows to be a book writer or some such and's here looking for things to put in one."

"Is anybody with her?" Roelich inquired, for what had possibly been the first attempts at spying had been discovered five days ago.

"Nope," Gormley answered. "Only, don't go getting no wrong ideas about seeing her walking around here after dark. She's not looking for company, and, way she put her knee into a cowhand's figured she needed it, she's set on not having any forced on her. Top of which, her husband's a captain in the Army down to Brownsville and'll be coming to collect her at the end of the month."

"Sounds like a gal to steer clear of," Roelich commented dryly, watching the woman disappear along the street. "This feller you told me about, did he come in on a hoss?"

"I reckon so," Gormley replied. "At least, it was Biggin from the livery barn's told me about him. Why?"

"No special reason." Roelich grunted, feeling no surprise that the peace officer had failed to try and learn what might have offered a clue to the newcomer's identity. Mounting his horse, before he set it moving, he went on, "Don't forget. If there's any shooting, don't let anybody go to look until they've had time to get it out of sight."

"I'll see to it," Gormley promised sullenly and, glaring malevolently at the other's departing back, continued under his breath, "You lousy son of a bitch. Happen you won't be so high and mighty after the Scanlon brothers get here."

Concluding his cryptic utterance the marshal slouched in the opposite direction to that taken by Roelich. However, his resentment at the hired gun's thinly disguised disdain was tempered by concern over the news he had been given. He had found his connection with Professor Morbeus most lucrative, particularly considering how little was expected of him in return for his services, so had no wish for anything to endanger it. If the thing should get by Petrov and Hooper, or have to be killed, that could happen. With such a contingency in mind he decided to wait at the Ranchero Saloon.* Oldest establishment of its kind, it was the last building on the street at the end from which the danger would come. As it restricted its entertainment to drinking, with no noisy distractions, it was ideal for his purpose.

* Named after the King and Kennedy steamboat *Ranchero,* which had played a leading part in the fighting at La Bolsa on February 4, 1860, between Captain—later Colonel, C.S.A.—John Salmon "Rip" Ford's company of Texas Rangers and Mexican guerrillas commanded by Juan "Cheno" Nepomuceno Cortina.—J.T.E.

Unaware of the peace officer's final comment, although he would certainly have questioned it if it had reached his ears, Roelich rode to the Man on the Wall Saloon. He glanced at the slender young woman in passing, but she showed no greater sign than previously of having any interest in him. As he came to a halt, he saw her enter the Premier Hotel, which faced his destination, and wondered if she was residing there. It did not seem likely, as the name was misleading and its rival establishment was superior in every respect except for being more expensive.

Putting the woman from his mind Roelich studied the saloon. A popular place with cowhands rather than those whose incomes were higher, it was clearly very busy. In fact, he was barely able to find sufficient room on either of the hitching rails to tether his horse. Having succeeded he crossed the sidewalk and, stepping through the batwing doors, paused on the threshold to study the surroundings.

There was no need for a new customer to speculate over the reason for the saloon's name. In general its furnishings and fittings were no different than would have been found in any similar establishment. However, fastened to the left side wall was a life-sized thick wooden shape like a man and covered with white paper. Behind the bar a notice announced, IF YOU FEEL LIKE SHOOTING, USE THE MAN ON THE WALL AND NOT THE OTHER CUSTOMERS OR MY FIXINGS. *Major Orville H. Tremaine, Texas Light Cavalry, Prop.* As the paper was unmarked, clearly none of the patrons had recently taken up the offer.

Having seen the target and read the notice on an earlier visit, Roelich ignored them. In spite of the barroom being well patronized, he had no difficulty in locating the reason for his coming there. A four-handed poker game was in progress at a table near the bar and one of its players matched Gormley's description better than any of the other customers.

Advancing and taking no notice of the curious glances being thrown at him from all sides, Roelich subjected the man in question to what should have been unobtrusive examination. However, he soon realized that his interest had not gone unnoticed by its subject. He also decided, not that he was surprised by the discovery, that most of the marshal's conclusions had been erroneous.

Bareheaded, with a black Texas-style Stetson hanging by its *barbiquejo* chin-strap from the back of his chair, the brown-haired young man's somewhat studious face was pallid; but this was caused by its skin being resistant to tanning by the sun and there was nothing weak or pasty about it. His thin hands seemed almost boneless, yet conveyed an impression of possessing strength and dexterity, particularly the latter, beyond average. While his garments were those of a cowhand, he wore them with ease that few dudes ever managed to display. Lastly, exposed by the right side of his jacket having been stitched back to allow unimpeded access to the ivory butt, the Army Colt hung just right—providing he could utilize the full potential of the excellently made contoured holster—for a real fast draw.

All in all, in spite of Gormley's unthinking dismissal, Roelich felt that the young newcomer merited further investigation. While it was probable that he had no connection with the, as yet, undetected watcher, his interest in the presence of hired guns suggested he was no casual visitor to the town. It could be that he was seeking employment in that line. Or he might be looking for one specific hired gun. In that case Roelich considered himself a possible candidate. After he had been compelled to shoot Joey Scanlon, the two older brothers had sworn to take revenge. From what he had heard, they were searching for him and could have taken on helpers in their quest.

There was, Roelich decided, one way in which he might be able to learn something about the pallid-faced young man without displaying his curiosity too obviously. He considered he was sufficiently experienced to bring it about.

"Howdy, gents. Is there room for another player?"

Three pairs of eyes turned to Roelich as he came to a halt

at the table and delivered his inquiry, the man in whom he was interested having continued to keep him under far from noticeable observation while he was approaching. There was a suggestion of suspicion in the trio's scrutiny. All were cowhands, two middle-aged and the other, somewhat more expensively dressed, in his late teens. Clearly even the youngster knew that he was not one of their kind and could probably guess at how he was employed. The older pair in particular were obviously wondering why he wished to join them. The stakes were moderate and there were other places in town at which he could have found a game with more wealthy opponents. However, they also realized he was not the kind who could be given a blank refusal.

"Stakes aren't high, mister," the oldest of the three said, in a way that showed neither welcome nor prohibition.

"That's the kind I go for," Roelich answered, adopting a relaxed and friendly tone. "Fact being, I'm not toting a whole bundle and that way it'll take me longer to lose it."

"We're allus willing to let a *loser* sit in," drawled the second of the middle-aged pair. "How about you-all, Doc?"

"I feel the same way," the pallid-faced young man replied, his voice that of a Texan who had had a good education. "Light and lose some, happen you've a mind, mister."

"Gracias," Roelich said, taking the chair opposite and watching the object of his interest as he introduced himself, but failing to detect any suggestion that his name meant anything.

"I'm Blinky. This here's Shuffles, and Lonny Tapper," the oldest player responded and, indicating the youngster, went on, "We ride for his pappy's Lazy Scissors spread."

"My name's Leroy," the young man announced, subjecting Roelich to just as keen a gaze. It was apparent that he, too, was wondering if his introduction had any significance for the newcomer. "On account of my daddy having been one and teaching me some about it, folks've got to calling me 'Doc.'"

"Pleased to meet you, gents," Roelich said, wondering in

what context he had heard of "Doc Leroy" and still studying the pallid, expressionless face. "Be right handy having you-all sit in, then, should one of these gents swoon through winning too many pots."

"Let's play poker!" Lonny Tapper put in impatiently. "Damn it, I'm down a whole ten simoleons already and I'm itching to get it back."

"Why, sure, we'll do that," Blinky promised with a tolerant air, taking up and riffling the cards thoroughly. He laid them before the newcomer and, looking pointedly at him, explained, "The game's straight five-card stud. No wild cards. No special hands like skip straights,* blazes,† nor whang-doodles,‡ and no limit—*within reason.*"

"That's fair enough, I'd say," Roelich assented, knowing from the emphasis on the last two words of the explanation he was being given a warning in case he had any ideas about leading the rancher's son into betting very high stakes.

"Then we'll get her on the trail," Blinky declared.

The cowhand's warning had been unnecessary, for Roelich was not in the game with such an intention. While talking, he had been conscious of the pallid-faced young man's continuous surreptitious scrutiny. It was apparent that the other still found him the source of speculation and he intended to learn why. Seeking the truth by direct means was

* Skip straight: a sequence such as Ace-3-5-7-9 not of the same suit, which when allowed beats two pair; i.e. 10-10-6-6-3.—J.T.E.

† Blaze: five picture cards, which would form at least a two-pair hand and in any combination beat a flush when being played. —J.T.E.

‡ Whang-doodle: actually a confidence trick. According to the story, a newcomer playing poker in a saloon was dealt ace, king, queen, jack, ten of hearts, which should have been unbeatable. However, on the showdown, an opponent with a two, three, four, five, and seven not even all in the same suit started to take in the pot after announcing he held a "whang-doodle." When the newcomer protested, he was shown a sign on a wall reading, NOTHING IN THIS HOUSE BEATS A WHANG-DOODLE. Accepting that this was a local rule, which varied from place to place, the newcomer continued playing. Later, he found himself holding a whang-doodle and bet heavily, confident that he must win. Instead, he was shown a second sign reading, ONLY ONE WHANG-DOODLE IS ALLOWED PER TABLE EACH NIGHT.—J.T.E.

almost certain to lead to trouble. However, there were ways to ask questions during a sociable game of poker that would otherwise be considered an unacceptable intrusion into private affairs. What was more, if he still felt dissatisfied with the results, he was confident that he could use another of the players to ascertain a matter of great importance.

If it should be necessary that Doc Leroy must be killed, either for personal reasons or because of a connection with his employer's business, Roelich wanted to know exactly what he would be up against.

CHAPTER THREE

HANDLE IT CAREFULLY

"All right, Lem, let's get moving. I reckon we've waited around for long enough," Tarbrush told his mule, having devoted about fifteen minutes to what he regarded as necessary watching and listening. While traveling alone and carrying out his solitary duties as a Nighthawk, he had developed the habit of speaking his thoughts aloud to his mount. Swinging on to the saddle, but keeping the Ballard single-shot carbine in his right hand, he gave the signal to start the animal walking. As he guided it in the required direction, he continued, "It don't seem like them fellers're coming back, and whatever it is's they don't want me to see hasn't showed up neither. Not that I'd've wanted it to, mind. Fact being, as long as we don't come across that fancy-dressed dude with the scary eyes, the sooner we get to Bannock's Ford, the better I'll like it."

Due to the three white men riding away from the young Negro, their conversation had become inaudible before he could discover how Hooper's suggestion had been received. They had now passed around a bend in the trail, which had taken them beyond his range of vision. In spite of Silkie Roelich's comments he considered that precautions were in order.

Dismounting, he had drawn the carbine from its saddle boot and had taken cover behind the trunk of the tree under which he had halted on hearing the trio approaching. While realizing that it would be necessary to reload by hand if he had to discharge the cartridge in the chamber, he found the seven-pounds weight of the weapon most comforting in his grasp. Having drawn the hammer from the half-cocked position of safety and set the mechanism at readiness, he had stood in silence to await developments.

As the seconds continued to drag by without incident, Tarbrush had concluded that Roelich and Petrov were not in favor of accepting their companion's proposition. However, he also considered that it might be inadvisable to follow them too closely. If he did, after having avoided accompanying them, they might decide that he had an undesirable interest in their affairs. Roelich would not need to consult with Hooper about how to handle such a contingency. With that in mind the young Negro elected to remain where he was until the trio were far ahead of him.

Even after Tarbrush was satisfied that the men did not intend to return, he kept the Ballard across the crook of his left arm. It had been obvious from the various comments they had made and the way in which the two westerners were carrying their rifles ready for use that they were searching for, or at least had reason to believe they might come across, something unusually dangerous. He was too intelligent to let himself be lulled into a sense of false security by remembering how Hooper had claimed that the color of his skin would prevent whatever they had been discussing from harming him. He had never heard of a grizzly bear that would differentiate between a Negro and a white man when on the rampage. Not that he believed such a creature was involved. In fact, he felt sure that Roelich's explanation was made to deter him from investigating if he should hear their quarry in the woodland.

Despite wondering what the mysterious creature might be, Tarbrush had no intention of trying to satisfy his curiosity. Nor, while sharing Roelich's sentiments regarding the limitations of his weapons, was he unduly worried by the possibility that it might be in the vicinity. The moon gave adequate light for him to see a fair way along the trail, but its effect upon the rest of his surroundings was largely nullified by the thickness of the foliage and undergrowth. He did not regard the latter as too grave a hazard. The nature of the terrain would render the silent passage of any large creature almost impossible and he felt sure that he could not be taken unawares. For one thing, he was not dependent solely upon his own resources for protection. The fifteen-hand mule by his side possessed exceptionally keen senses that made it an ideal ally under the circumstances. Clearly it appreciated his disquieted feelings. It was equally tense and alert.

Apart from the usual sounds to be expected in woodland at night, the young Negro heard nothing. Nor, although its long ears were pricked and it constantly looked around with nostrils testing the air, did the mule's behavior suggest that it was detecting any cause for alarm. So, by the time Tarbrush was ready to move on, he was convinced that the mysterious creature was not close enough to worry over.

In spite of his summations Tarbrush did not relax his vigilance when he started the mule moving. Trusting it implicitly he allowed it to carry him along the trail with the minimum of guidance on his part. However, he gradually began to throw off the premonition of evil, which—although he did not know it—had mainly been created by his misgivings where Petrov was concerned. Everything remained so peaceful that, after he had covered almost a mile without any disturbance, he returned the Ballard's hammer to half cock and, replacing it in his saddle boot, relaxed. Then he came upon a sight which diverted the last of his thoughts from the gloomy forebodings that had been assailing him.

After having passed through an area of particularly dense undergrowth that reduced visibility to a minimum, Tarbrush found that he had reached a point where the thickly growing bushes were broken by a fair-sized clearing. Glancing around the patch of open land, which extended to what was clearly a backwater of the Rio Grande, he found that it was occupied. However, the occupants were not the hard-faced trio who had been responsible for his earlier apprehensions. Nor, he felt sure, could they in any way be connected with whatever kind of dangerous creature had caused the three men to behave in such a wary and—as far as the young Negro was concerned—worrying fashion.

Standing unhitched in the center of the clearing, a plump brown horse that had passed its prime as a draft animal was cropping leisurely at the springy grass alongside a dilapidated and empty buckboard. Beyond it a big, thickset, and elderly white man wearing a battered straw hat, a collarless white shirt, patched bib-overalls, and town-dweller's boots was fishing on the edge of the backwater with every evidence of success. A large oaken bucket and a wicker hamper were at his right side and he was using two poles, each about ten feet in length. One of them was resting on a forked stick that was thrust into the bank to his left and extended so that its line was dangling into the water. Tucked under his right arm the second was bowed over and jerking in concert with the movements of what was clearly some powerful force beneath the river's surface.

A keen fisherman, the young Negro found the sight to be of considerable interest. It was one that he could not pass by. However, even as he was about to halt and watch, the pole on the rest was subjected to a sudden and violent jerk.

Tall, bulky, and—as became apparent from his scanty white hair when the hat was sent flying from his head—elderly though the man on the bank might be, he proved to be capable of moving with considerable rapidity. Letting out an explosively profane comment, which Tarbrush considered was excusable under the circumstances, he lunged sideways. Taking his left hand from the pole it had been helping to control, he made a grab for and managed to catch the other as it was being wrenched from its rest. Although he was successful in preventing it from being dragged into the water, his troubles were not yet at an end.

Taking in the scene with a comprehensive glance the young Negro could appreciate and sympathize with the other man's predicament. Being pinned firmly between his right elbow and ribs, he could keep the first pole held at an angle that allowed its tip to absorb much of the strain that was being placed upon it. There was no such security where the second pole was concerned. While he had contrived to grasp it about eighteen inches above the bottom of its butt and was managing to raise the upper end, the leverage being exerted by whatever had taken his bait was too great for him to be able to retain it in that position. Furthermore, even if he succeeded, it was unlikely that he could keep the two fish apart and prevent them from tangling, then breaking, the lines.

Tarbrush needed barely five seconds of consideration to decide how he could best assist the elderly white man. Instead of stopping the mule as he had intended and remaining a passive spectator, he delivered a tap with his heels and a signal via the bit to send it across the clearing at a swift trot. Going by the horse and buckboard he did not even wait for his mount to halt. Instead, he quit the saddle and released the split-ended reins. Listening to as fine a flow of profanity as it had ever been his privilege to hear, he darted forward secure in the knowledge that allowing them to dangle free would "ground-hitch" the mule as effectively as if he had stayed to fasten it to some immovable object. As he was approaching, he noticed that the voice—in spite of the speaker's well-worn clothing and far from impressive means of transport—was that of a man who hailed from somewhere south of the Mason-Dixon line other than Texas, and who had had a good education.

"Here, sir," the young Negro said, arriving alongside the fisherman as the second pole was being dragged out to his arm's length. He realized there was no time to spare if they were to avert a disaster. "Let me take that 'n' for you-all."

At the first sound of another human being's voice, the elderly man snapped his head around. He had been so engrossed in trying to cope with his dilemma that he was oblivious of all else and unaware of Tarbrush's fortuitous arrival.

However, despite his florid and amiable features—or as much of them as could be seen behind a nicotine-stained white mustache of enormous proportions—registering surprise, he did not hesitate for an instant before surrendering the pole that was causing the difficulty.

"Thank you kindly, young feller," the man said, in tones redolent of relief mingled with gratitude, swiftly returning his left hand to the task from which it had been diverted. "But handle it carefully, though. There's a real big and strong one on the line."

Without bothering to respond verbally to the advice Tarbrush manipulated the pole until the butt was safely positioned beneath his right armpit and he held it in both hands. On raising the tip tentatively he silently conceded that the man's summation was correct. The pole bent into a graceful arc, and although there was no sign of the fish as yet—other than the vigorous swirling motions where the taut line disappeared into the water—he was conscious of its forceful tugging and solid weight as it struggled against the restraint.

Even as Tarbrush began to revel in the prospect of dealing with such a worthwhile adversary, he became aware of something that made him think of the man's comment. In the past he had frequently caught fish of considerable size, weight, and strength. However, his conquests had always been accomplished with the aid of a suitable branch cut on the way to the Brazos River. With a sense of consternation he discovered that he was now handling a much more sophisticated device.

The pole in the young Negro's hands consisted of a single piece of bamboo, which had been carefully prepared for fishing. After it had been seasoned, each joint had been skilfully heated and straightened. Then, after the knots had been scraped down, it was whipped along its length with black silk and varnished. To facilitate gripping it a cork handle about twenty-four inches long was attached at the butt. Although the finished product was pleasant to look at, it seemed very fragile after the kind of pole to which he was accustomed, and he could envisage that its owner would be highly displeased if he caused it to be damaged.

Apart from the latter consideration Tarbrush would have had no doubt that he could cope. Although much lighter and elegant the tackle was almost identical to that with which he had spent many happy and fruitful hours in the past. The line was lashed directly to a metal ring on the tip of the pole and there was no reel that would have allowed more of it to be paid out and so relieve some of the strain. Not that he gave a thought to the omission, having only rarely seen and never used such a device. However, even while employing his usual variety of sturdy pole and line, there had been numerous occasions when it would have been detrimental to them if he had tried to haul a heavy and freshly hooked fish from the water. Instead, he had been compelled to raise, lower, or make other alterations to the direction in which the pole was pointing as a means of playing his powerful quarry until it was sufficiently tired to be landed without the tackle being broken.

Alarmed at seeing the pole was taking on a curve that would have caused any other he had handled to buckle or snap, Tarbrush hurriedly lowered it. The instant the pressure was reduced, it began to straighten. In itself this did not surprise him. Even an ordinary branch had a certain amount of pliancy, although none had ever responded with such alacrity.

Noticing that his actions had allowed the line to slacken, Tarbrush's instinctive reaction was to correct it. On being lifted the pole once again took on a bend. However, he grew exhilarated rather than concerned as he felt the springy resilience fighting against the strain. He realized that the treatment it had received was enhancing the bamboo's natural resilience and strength. Provided he was not too heavy handed, it would suffer no harm from the fish's struggles. Comforted by the discovery he gave his attention to the task of playing his quarry to exhaustion.

"Lordy lord!" the young Negro said, after close to two

minutes of effort, glancing around for the first time. The elderly man had moved away so there was no danger of their lines becoming entangled, and was displaying an equal dexterity in controlling the vigorous movements of his pole. "This here's one tolerable good fighting fish."

"Mine's not exactly climbing out to make it easy for me," the owner of the poles pointed out, and sensing that he was addressing a kindred spirit, his huge moustache bristled jovially as he went on, "Which I'm willing to bet he's bigger than that one you're having so much trouble bringing in."

"I dunno about that, sir," Tarbrush contradicted with a grin, as he looked to where his quarry was struggling weakly just below the surface. "Anyways, seeing's I ain't greedy, this'n's big enough for lil ole me when I'm using such a fancy pole."

Even as he was speaking, Tarbrush found he was faced with a dilemma. From all appearances the fight was just about over. Usually he would have been able to either beach or lift his catch from the water. In this case, as the bank rose almost two feet above the surface, the former was impossible. Nor, impressed as he had been by its powers of resistance, did he want to attempt lifting with the elegant pole. He decided to wait and find out how his companion dealt with the problem.

The wait was not prolonged. Almost as soon as Tarbrush had reached his decision, the elderly man thrust the butt of the pole backward. Deftly allowing it to slip through and be supported by his left hand, he caught the line with his right. A quick heave plucked the fish from the water and sent it to flop well clear of the edge of the bank.

"You're taking your time, aren't you?" the man inquired, although he could guess why the young Negro was doing so. "If an old jasper like me can fetch a fish out, a feller your age should be able to."

"I could've some time back," Tarbrush answered. "Only, I've never used such a fancy pole and didn't want to take a chance on busting it."

"That's mighty considerate of you, even if unnecessary," the man declared, laying down his pole. "But, seeing's you feel that way, bring him over and I'll land him for you-all."

"He'll go about five–six pounds, I reckon," Tarbrush estimated, having guided his catch around so that the elderly man could grasp the line and swing it ashore. Studying the fish for a moment, he continued, "I figured he was a cat, but he looks a mite different to any blue or flathead I ever caught."

"We don't get either in this part of the Rio Grande," the white angler replied. "He's a channel catfish. They don't grow as big as blues and flatheads,* but I think, living in faster and cleaner water as they do, they fight a whole heap better and are choicer eating too." His gaze went briefly from the fish to the river, then studied the young Negro in a speculative manner, and he continued, "Are you headed for Bannock's?"

"Why, sure," Tarbrush confirmed, setting down the pole carefully. "I'm looking to get took on as a Nighthawk with a trail drive."

"There're at least three outfits around, so you might not have to wait too long," the man went on. "But I don't reckon all the chores will be taken before morning. Are you in any all-fired rush to get there?"

"Not specially," Tarbrush admitted, guessing what was coming.

"Well, it's this way," the man explained, justifying the young Negro's hopes. "I've been baiting this hole up for over a week and there'll be plenty more like these two old fiddlers† waiting to be caught. What say we get the hooks out and then, happen it's not against your religious beliefs,

* An example of the sizes to which the blue, *Ictalurus furcatus,* and flathead, or yellow, *Pylodictis olivaris,* subspecies of catfish can grow under favorable conditions is given in THE HIDE AND TALLOW MEN.—J.T.E.

† Fiddler, colloquial name for the channel catfish, *Ictalurus punctatus.* —J.T.E.

'we'll have us a bottle of cold beer, a bite to eat, and see if we can't oblige them."

"It's right neighborly of you-all to offer, sir," Tarbrush enthused. "And any time I get me a religion that says I can't take me a beer, specially when it's cold, I'll right soon make a change. How'll it be was I to get the hooks out and leave you-all to tend to the beer?"

"That's what I'd call an equitable division of labor," the elderly man conceded, waving a hand toward the hamper. "Those will help you."

Stepping forward Tarbrush looked at the two objects that had so far gone unobserved. One was a stout round piece of wood about eighteen inches long, the purpose of which he knew; but he was unable to decide to what use he was expected to put the other. It was a flat bone about a foot in length and with a V-shaped cleft cut at one end. After dispatching the fishes with blows on the head from the stick, he turned his gaze to where his companion was drawing up a net containing four bottles of beer that had been suspended on a string, again unnoticed.

"I hates to sound ignorant, even when I am," Tarbrush declared, dropping the stick and taking up the bone, "but what's this doohickey for?"

"It's something an English friend taught me to make and use," the man explained. "He called it a disgorger.* Slide the notch down the line to the hook and you'll fetch it out a whole heap quicker and easier than opening him up."

Carrying out the instructions Tarbrush was pleased with the result. As was usually the case, the catfish had taken the hooks well down their throats before being impaled. When this had happened in the past, he had always had to gut his catch and cut the line to retrieve the hook.

"Whooee!" Tarbrush grinned, accepting an open bottle at the conclusion of his task. "Now I've seen how easy that dee

* Pronounced "de-gorge"—J.T.E.

—whatever you call it makes getting the hooks out, what say we catches some more to use it on?"

"Why not," agreed the old man, realizing that he was in the company of a fellow angling enthusiast who was eager for the feel of the well-made pole in action again. "I don't know how you feel about them, but there are some big old night crawlers in the bucket juicy enough to keep the fiddlers coming."

"I've always done right well with 'em," Tarbrush replied, knowing that some fishermen preferred other baits. " 'Cepting when I was after some li'l ole pan fish."

"Then dip in and help yourself," the elderly man offered. "We'll eat after we've brought in a few."

Accepting the invitation Tarbrush dug a hand into the damp moss that had been placed in the bucket to keep its occupants alive and in good condition. Selecting a night crawler he drew it out and carefully impaled it upon the hook. When it was positioned to his satisfaction, he picked up the rod and swung the wriggling creature into the water as near as he could manage to where the line had disappeared beneath the surface on his arrival. Nor, such was the effectiveness of the earlier baiting carried out by the elderly man, did he have long to wait for a bite.

Almost an hour went by pleasantly, with each of the anglers taking three more catfish that were about the same size as the original captures. In addition Tarbrush found out that his host, Gollicker by name, was the local doctor, and he was offered accommodation for himself and his mount after the fishing was over.

Once again, just as the doctor was suggesting that they stop for a meal, both had a fish take at the same time. What was more, each could tell that it was his largest catch so far. Such was their rowdy enthusiasm as they played the powerful quarry that their entire attention was engaged.

Neither was aware that the mule was looking toward the

bushes on the upstream side of the clearing and becoming restless!

Nor that the foliage was being agitated by something large, but as yet concealed, thrusting its way through!

CHAPTER FOUR

I DON'T LIKE THE WAY YOU PLAY!

"Would this be the first time you Lazy Scissors boys've been to Bannock's Ford?" Silkie Roelich inquired, paying a waiter who had delivered the round of beers he had ordered after winning the first pot in which he had participated.

Speaking in an amiably casual fashion the hired gun was paving the way for gaining information about the only player in whom he was interested. Such a question was entirely permissible under the rules of conduct that had come into being west of the Mississippi River, allowing the person to whom it was addressed to decide how far he wanted to go in answering. It also showed no interest in anything of a purely personal or confidential nature.

"It sure is," Blinky agreed, and looked around the Man on the Wall Saloon's barroom before continuing, "Mind you, I'm a small-town boy myself. So I wouldn't cotton to living here with all the coming 'n' going."

"Good health to you, even though you did promise's how you-all was going to lose," Shuffles drawled, raising his schooner and, having taken a drink, went on, "Way ole Blinky's disrespecting it, I sure hope this ain't your hometown."

"It's not," Roelich confirmed, knowing that he, too, was being asked indirectly for information and turning it to his advantage. Although addressing the cowhand, he was looking from the corner of his eye at the pallid-featured young man who was sitting on the opposite side of the table. "I'm working for Professor Morbeus down on Mission Island."

"Heard some talk of it," Blinky commented, wiping beer froth from his mouth.

Although the oldest member of the Lazy Scissors trio sounded as if he was not in favor of what he had heard, Roelich was uninterested in the reaction. However, the hired gun found himself unable to decide whether reference to his employment had had any effect upon Doc Leroy.

"Aw, hell!" Lonny Tapper exclaimed, putting down his half-emptied schooner with a thump and wriggling impatiently on his chair. "Are we playing poker, or going to sit whittle-whanging?"

"You'll have to excuse him, gents," Blinky drawled, glancing at the players who did not belong to the Lazy Scissors ranch. There was just a hint of apology in his voice, for the youngster's words had been far from tactful and might be resented by a man like the hired gun. "He's just keen to let you-all do some of that losing you was talking about, Silkie."

"Then we'd best get to doing it," Roelich answered.

The conversation had been progressing satisfactorily, but the hired gun was too wise to make it obvious that he wanted it continued. Instead, confident that he could resume it along the desired lines, he accepted the interruption with no sign of disapproval.

Roelich's failure to detect any response from the enigmatic young man made him even more determined to succeed. Nor was he motivated by mere idle curiosity. Added to what he had been told by Marshal Arthur Gormley, his every instinct suggested that the other's presence in Bannock's Ford was in some way connected with himself, or the work he was hired to carry out. So, whichever it should be, and in spite of knowing that a potentially grave matter had brought him into the town, he considered there was sufficient justification for him to remain where he was until he had learned more about Doc Leroy.

"After all," the hired gun thought, as Shuffles began to

deal the cards, "There wasn't anything to point to that damned thing coming this way. If it does, Petrov and Hooper'll stop it one way or the other. And should it come to shooting and Leroy is interested in what's doing out to the island, he's one jasper who *mustn't* be let see it."

"I allus did like a feller's keeps his word," Tapper announced cheerfully as the showdown established he had beaten Roelich's hand. Then he glanced at Doc Leroy and went on, "And one who ain't scared to stay in."

"You give *me* some cards and I'll stay in," Blinky declared, deliberately misinterpreting what amounted to a provocative and even insulting comment.

"Are you-all fixing to set up as a doctor down here, Doc?" Roelich inquired, using the altercation between the youngster and the old cowhand as an excuse to restart the conversation, as though he was trying to smooth things over by changing the subject.

"I've never qualified as a doctor," the young man replied, and although his face remained impassive, there was an undertone of bitterness to his otherwise matter-of-fact drawl.

Once again, the hired gun's efforts were thwarted by Tapper. Gathering up the cards hurriedly in his eagerness to get on with the game, the youngster gave them only a perfunctory shuffling before setting them in front of Blinky to be cut.* However, Roelich still gave no sign of irritation over the further delay.

When the hand had been played out, the hired gun found himself unable to achieve his purpose. While Doc Leroy displayed no hostility, nor any other emotion that could be determined, he was obviously disinclined to discuss his affairs. Nor could Roelich think of any way to make him do so without risking a confrontation. Having no wish to do that until he was better informed about the stranger, he allowed the subject to lapse and went on with the game. His primary

* The convention in the majority of card games is that the deal is in a right-hand direction and the man at the dealer's left side cuts the deck. —J.T.E.

objective had come to nothing, but he felt sure that he could bring his secondary purpose to fruition.

One of the things a man who earned his living through his skill with a gun and an accomplished poker player had in common was the ability to assess the quality of the opposition. Being both, Roelich had developed such an aptitude. Only half a dozen pots were needed for him to conclude that the three older men he was up against were efficient contenders, the—for him at least—moderate stakes notwithstanding. Although lacking some of the major refinements in tactics and mathematics pertaining to the game, Blinky and Shuffles were cagy players. They placed their bets wisely and rarely overestimated the potential value of their hands.*

Capable as the pair were, it was soon obvious to Roelich that Doc Leroy was even better. In addition to displaying a *very* thorough knowledge of the mathematics and tactics, he had that most essential requisite of a poker "wolf," patience. Folding on the arrival of his first exposed card unless he had either an ace or a pair "back to back,"† except for an infrequent "sociable" hand to prevent the other players from detecting his system, he was content to play only when the odds were substantially in his favor. Such tactics were invariably successful in the long run and did not produce spectacular short-term results. They were also a source of irritation to the class of contender—known to their superiors as "lambs"—who believed that winning at poker was dependent solely upon that mystical quality called luck.

That Tapper belonged to the lamb category was equally plain to the hired gun. Where Doc Leroy in particular would fold as soon as the cards he was holding were beaten—for example, if another player received a higher pair than those

* A description of the "hands" in a game of poker and their relative value to each other is given in Two Miles to the Border.—J.T.E.

† Back to back: when the first two cards dealt are of the same denomination. In stud poker the first, "hole," card is dealt face down and the rest, usually four, face up. A more detailed explanation of the game is given in Cold Deck, Hot Lead.—J.T.E.

with which he had stayed in the pot—no matter how many more were to come, the youngster would continue to play and hope for an improvement. Only rarely did he improve his holding by the arrival of advantageous cards. Mostly he would have been advised to get out and avoid any further squandering of his money.

Studying Tapper's style of play and demeanor as the game progressed, Roelich grew even more confident that he could produce the situation he wanted. With this end in mind he forgot his training as a wolf and played far more recklessly than he would have in different circumstances. Although it was costing him money, everything else appeared to be going in his favor.

While skill was always the deciding factor in the game of stud poker, to a certain degree luck would effect the outcome. Even the shrewdest wolf could only win when he was called if he had the best hand, which he mostly had should the pot reach that point, but he knew how to keep his losses to a minimum.

That evening, fortune did not smile on Tapper. On the rare occasions when he held a hand that ought to have proved lucrative, not once did all the other players go all the way with him. Despite his best efforts he had poor control of his emotions. Nor did his invariable habit of betting high when bluffing, and low in the hope of inducing his opponents to carry on against a powerful hand (particularly as in the former case he insisted upon displaying that he had brought off a successful bluff) improve his chances. However, like every lamb, he failed to comprehend the reasons for his misfortunes. Instead, he only noticed the benefits being accrued by Doc Leroy's skillful methods. In addition to his highly effective tactics the pallid-faced young man was enjoying a moderate streak of luck that was making him the game's winner.

That only three players were involved to any extent in his rare successful hands did not go unmentioned by Tapper. In fact, after just over an hour of play, his continued disparaging comments on the subject were drawing disturbed and disapproving looks from his father's employees.

With each display of petulance by the youngster Roelich hoped that the situation he wanted would arise. However, the man at whom the complaints and thinly veiled insults were directed showed no sign of resentment. Instead, he continued to play with the same relentless and ruthless efficiency. Nor was the hired gun able to speed up the process by causing Tapper to become drunk on hard liquor, his suggestions of a change from beer meeting with a unanimous refusal.

Watching the fingers creeping around the face of the clock behind the bar, Roelich began to grow increasingly impatient. As yet there had been nothing to suggest that the two men he had left to keep watch on the woodland might be in need of his assistance. For all that, being conscientious and loyal to his employer, he was not entirely reconciled to having left them unsupervised. Petrov was able to control the creature that had escaped when in the confines of the Island Mission, but the same might not apply under prevailing conditions. As an added source of concern Roelich doubted whether Hooper could be relied upon to behave sensibly in an emergency. So, much as he tried to reassure himself with the thought that he was occupied more advantageously in investigating and, if necessary, dealing with the man called Doc Leroy, he still felt perturbed by the delay in rejoining his companions.

"Here's the good ole king of clubs for you-all, Lonny," Shuffles announced, dealing the first of the "up" cards while Roelich was considering how to take a more active line in forcing the issue. The cowhand was speaking with a forced cheerfulness in an attempt to smooth over the youngster's latest petulant outburst. "Try this here nine of spades, Doc. Can't do no better'n the five of diamonds for you-all, Silkie. Could be you'll find the seven of clubs useful, Blinky. But I'm damned if I know what good this li'l ole deuce of spades is to me. King to open."

"I reckon I'll give her a whirl with a whole dollar," Tapper said, having the ace of clubs in the hole and trying none too successfully to sound nonchalant.

"I'll see that," Doc Leroy drawled, with a complete lack of emotion, but he tossed six silver dollars into the pot. "And raise it another five."

"That's too rich for my blood," Roelich stated, pushing his two cards toward the center of the table.

Following what they considered to be an excellent example set by the hired gun, the two older cowhands also folded their cards and withdrew from the pot. Since the game started, each had developed a profound respect for the pallid-faced young man's capabilities. On his past performance he had at least an ace in the hole, or—more probably—the support of another nine. So far, when holding strong cards, he had always raised the betting. Bumping up the pot might drive out other players, but he realized that the more who stayed in, the greater became the chances of somebody being dealt a hand to beat him. Being a true and practising wolf, he was content to settle for smaller and more certain gains.

"Here's the ace of hearts for you-all, Lonny," Shuffles said, after the youngster had covered the raise without a moment's hesitation or consideration. "And the ten of clubs to you, Doc. Ace-king t—!"

"Five simoleons!" Tapper interrupted, feeding the pot eagerly and delighted by the way his hand was shaping.

"And another five," Doc Leroy countered.

"And five more!"

"Yours and five on top of it."

Studying the cards in play, which was more than their inexperienced companion thought of doing, Blinky and Shuffles were relieved when he merely covered and did not reraise. Roelich watched carefully. His instincts as a poker player suggested that the kind of situation he was hoping for might be in the making.

As Tapper drew the three of clubs and his opponent received the nine of the same suit, the other men considered that he had been well advised not to have taken the betting any higher, no matter what his hole card might be.

"Pair to bet," Shuffles intoned, a slightly worried note creeping into his voice at the thought of what the two exposed nines might portend.

"Ten li'l ole iron men," Doc Leroy obliged, extracting a bill of that denomination from the pile in front of him.

Tapper did not respond immediately. This was the first time he had been expected to put up such a large sum in a single raise. He began to feel a slight stirring of alarm as he remembered the other's hitherto extremely cautious play. The only occasions when Doc Leroy had betted heavily was when he held a powerful hand.

"I—I'll see that," the youngster said at last, somewhat indecisively, counting out the required amount and trying to ignore an inner voice that insisted upon reminding him that three nines licked a pair of aces to a frazzle. Silently praying for either of the remaining aces to come his way, his hand shook a little as he took a drink from his almost empty schooner and tried to speak cheerfully. "I'll buy the next round out of my w—!"

"King of hearts, Lonny," Shuffles put in, turning and flipping the card across. His concern became even more noticeable, much as he tried to hide it, when he saw what he was dealing to the other player. "Nine of spades, Doc. Two pairs to bet."

The pale and studious features of the young man were devoid of any expression as his mouth opened to say, "Twenty dollars."

"Tw-tw—!" Tapper croaked, drawing little comfort from the knowledge that the two pairs he was holding far outranked the nines and tens that were exposed to his gaze.

Silence fell on the table as the youngster looked around as if in search of guidance. Although his two companions wished that they could supply advice, their sense of fair play, as much as an awareness of what might happen if they did, prevented either from doing so. Each felt sure that Doc Leroy had a third nine in the hole, but all they could do was sit still and hope their employer's son would reach the right decision.

Failing to learn anything from the two older cowhands, Tapper turned his eyes to his opponent. While the pot was the largest of the session and Doc Leroy had more of his money at stake than in any other, for all the apprehension he showed, he might have been doing no more than idling his time.

There was, the youngster concluded after a few seconds' study, an air of complete confidence and assurance about the man against whom he was playing. If so, it could only be caused by one thing. He was holding a full house of three nines and two tens—which left two pairs, even aces and kings, far to the rear.

Only two courses were open to Tapper. Either he called and bet and had a showdown (in his opinion raising it was out of the question) or he must fold and concede the pot.

Neither alternative was attractive!

Doing the former would cost a whole twenty dollars, which was almost all Tapper had left of the money he had brought with him. If—as he was growing increasingly certain when he thought of how his opponent had played up to that point—the other's hole card should be nine, the sum would disappear along with what he had already staked.

After another thirty seconds the youngster reached a bitter decision. Turning over his hole card with a gesture of exasperation, he glared at it for a moment. Then, slamming it onto the table furiously, he spat out two words.

"I'm in!"

Soft sighs of relief and approval broke from the two older cowhands. In their opinion, no matter how galling Tapper must have found it having to concede the pot, he had acted in the only sensible fashion. Each of them felt sure that, if he had followed his usual practice of calling Doc Leroy's final bet, he would merely have been throwing good money after bad.

Despite having formed a different summation of the situation, Roelich was just as satisfied with the way things had turned out. He also realized that, even providing his assumptions were correct, his purpose was not yet fully achieved. For it to come to fruition the annoyed and disappointed youngster must find out what had happened to him.

There, the hired gun told himself, lay the fly in the ointment.

Being an active practitioner in the art of poker wolfdom, Doc Leroy would not display the exact contents of his winning hand of his own volition.

Unlike the lamb category of player, who always felt the need to impress the rest of the participants in the game with his skill, courage, and brilliance, a wolf *never* permitted *anybody* to see his hole card unless the other had paid for the privilege. When the lamb had pulled off a coup, he wanted the fact to be appreciated. Not so the wolf. He cared nothing for the acclaim of his opponents while the game was in progress and considered that the less they knew about his methods and tactics, the greater were his chances of success.

With that wolfish trait in mind Roelich reached out and started to gather up the cards. Previously Tapper had done this in his desire to commence another pot, but he was now sitting and gazing as if mesmerized at the black nines and tens. Such a reaction was ideal for the hired gun's purpose. It gave him an excuse for what he meant to do. While picking up the winning hand, as if by accident, he flipped the hole card over and it fluttered back, exhibited for all to see, face uppermost to the table.

It was—the *deuce of diamonds!*

Blinky and Shuffles let out muted gasps of mingled astonishment and admiration. By his complete reversal of tactics Doc Leroy had hoodwinked them as thoroughly as his oppo-

46

nent. Each considered he had seen a magnificent example of how a bluff should be performed.

From all appearances Tapper did not share his companions' sentiments. Rather he sat looking as if he could not credit the evidence of his eyes. Although they had been removed by Roelich, he could still visualize the nine of spades, ten of clubs, nine of clubs, and ten of spades with which he had been confronted. Now, its red pips forming a vivid contrast, he was staring at a card that was neither the nine of hearts or diamonds that he had been convinced was in the hole. So he had conceded a good pot to a two-pair hand of lower value than that which he had held. Nor did he take any comfort from the evidence that his older and vastly more experienced companions had also been taken in by the subterfuge.

"Well, I'll swan!" Roelich exclaimed, slapping the top of the table with his left hand. He had anticipated something of the kind was taking place, but wanted to rub salt into the youngster's wounded ego. "You-all sure's hell fell for that, Lonny!"

Already burning with indignation and humiliation at having allowed himself to be bluffed, the words acted like a goad to Tapper.

"God damn it!" the youngster yelled, glaring at Doc Leroy and leaping to his feet with such violence that he sent his chair flying backward. Lifting his right hand until it was hovering over the butt of his far from efficiently holstered Army Colt, he continued to splutter furiously, "I don't like the way you play!"

Although the pallid-featured young man remained seated, Blinky and Shuffles rose with expressions of alarm. Like the hired gun, they had noticed the way in which Doc Leroy was armed and knew what this might portend. Furthermore, if various stories they had heard were true, he possessed a skill that far exceeded the limited ability of their employer's son, where handling firearms was concerned.

Watching the developments Roelich was delighted by

what he saw. In his present frame of mind Tapper was liable to say or do something that would provoke gunplay. What was more, the other two cowhands were almost certain to come to his aid against the older and clearly more competent man. In which case the hired gun's dilemma with regard to Doc Leroy might be resolved without any further effort on his own part.

No matter how skilled the pallid young man proved to be, he was unlikely to survive a shootout against odds of three to one.

CHAPTER FIVE

HE MUST'VE SEEN IT

"Whee-doggie!" Tarbrush whooped, filled with the heady exhilaration of a dedicated angler who was tangling with a large, powerful, and most satisfying adversary. "This here's just about the fightingest son of a bitch I've come up against, 'cluding bigmouths. But I reckon I'm getting the best of him."

"That so?" asked Doctor Gollicker, sweating profusely from the effort he had been putting into an equally strenuous tussle with the big channel catfish that was now turning on its side at the end of his line. "Well, I'm willing to bet I'll whip mine and get it onto the bank before you can. Not," he continued with the cagy instinct of a poker wolf laying a trap for an opponent, "that he's anywheres close to being finished just yet, but I feel lucky."

With the struggles of his quarry growing weaker and his companion's words coming to his ears, although up to that point he had been absorbed in his sport to the exclusion of all else, Tarbrush suddenly became aware that his big brown mule—which he had offsaddled when he was invited to continue fishing—was no longer grazing peacefully. Even as the realization was making itself felt, the animal threw back its head and let out a snort of alarm.

Knowing that his mount only behaved in such a manner when it detected something of a disturbing nature, the young Negro wondered what was causing the reaction. The fun he had been having while fishing had driven away the last of the misgivings caused by the meeting with the three white men. So he did not connect the way in which the mule was acting with the matter they had been discussing. However, trusting the animal not to raise a false alarm, he looked in the direction that it was watching. Noticing that the bushes on the upstream edge of the clearing were being shaken violently, he was not kept waiting for long before he was able to ascertain the cause.

The shape that thrust itself into view and started to approach the anglers was human, exceptionally large, and black. Even without the unexpected nature of his arrival his whole appearance was startling, frightening even.

Naked except for a pair of ancient and ragged trousers, the newcomer's height was well in excess of six feet and augmented by a truly massive muscular development. Taken with his body's bulk his other features contrived to make him look even more gigantic and horrific. His completely hairless head, which had lost one ear, topped the wide shoulders without seeming to be supported by a neck. Broad, short, and broken, his nose flared almost like the nostrils of a wild animal above an open and noiselessly snarling mouth. Some of his teeth were no more than jagged stumps. Those that remained whole had been filed to points after the fashion of certain African tribes that practised cannibalism. Walking in a swift, flatfooted manner, his arms dangled loosely by his sides instead of swinging in concert with the movement of his legs. A band of metal with a broken link of chain attached to it, discolored and almost indistinguishable against his skin, encircled each wrist. The fingers of his enormous hands were constantly flexing as if seeking to grasp and crush something.

Awesome as the general aspect of the huge Negro's face and physique might be, his eyes made it infinitely more so. Wide open and with not a vestige of brow above them, there was something chilling about their unwinking stare. It was as if there was no conscious life behind them and that he was completely devoid of all human emotions.

"Land's sakes!" Tarbrush shouted, staring in amazement at the apparition. After removing the mule's saddle he had changed positions with his companion and so was the nearer of them to the newcomer. "Where in hell did you come from, friend, and what's ailing you-all?"

Knowing nothing of the mule's abilities Gollicker had paid no attention to the change in its behavior. On hearing the young Negro's startled exclamation he glanced around. For a moment his gaze returned to the front without having taken in all that he had seen. Then his head snapped back to carry out what would come to be known as a "double take."

At first the elderly white man could hardly believe the evidence of his eyes. No Negroes lived in the vicinity of Bannock's Ford. A few were employed on the King and Kennedy riverboats, but he felt sure that the newcomer was not one of them. One would not readily forget seeing such a person. In fact, Gollicker was reminded of the illustration of an ogre he had seen in a book of fairy stories he had given to his grandson as a Christmas present. Then his professional instincts took command and he threw off the fanciful notion. That was a human being approaching, but not one who was in a normal state of mind. Nor was the shambling gait and general demeanor induced merely by an overindulgence in ardent spirits. It must have come through the taking of some form of narcotics.

One thing was apparent to the doctor. The situation was fraught with peril. If the newcomer should be bent on mischief, which seemed very likely, his huge size and obvious strength would make him a formidable antagonist. Furthermore, being in such a mental condition he would not be amenable to reason.

Tarbrush duplicated his companion's summation of the danger, if in a less clinical and scientific fashion. Briefly, the conclusions he drew caused him to freeze into immobility. While he was far from being the easily frightened comic "darkie" who had already become a regular character on the stage, he was conditioned by generations of a superstitious lore filled with tales of unearthly creatures in human form. It was only by exerting all his willpower that he managed to break free from the sense of nameless dread that had been produced by the huge man's appearance.

In spite of his misgivings Tarbrush did not at first give a thought to the Navy Colt in his waistband. He knew how to use it, but had neither the instincts nor the training of a gunfighter and had never found cause to turn it against another human being. When he finally decided that it might be advisable to arm himself, he had left it too late to do so.

Even as Tarbrush dropped the fishing pole and made a grab at the revolver's butt, the other Negro's hands shot out with remarkable speed for one so bulky and closed on his shoulders. Their grip was so powerful that his whole body felt numbed and he was helpless to resist. From his rear Gollicker shouted something; but the pain that was being inflicted upon him prevented him from making out what was being said. Instead, all he was aware of were the two terrible staring eyes glaring at him. Then he was lifted from the ground. With a twist of the torso his captor hurled him aside with no more apparent effort than if he were a baby and not a full grown man.

Such was the awesome strength with which the young Negro's assailant propelled him that he was sent for some distance before his feet touched the ground. Nor, on alighting, had he the slightest control over his limbs. Carried onward by the irresistible impetus, which also caused him to pirouette helplessly, he flailed wildly with his arms and tried to regain some form of governance over his movements.

In the course of the turn that finally saw Tarbrush's balance completely destroyed, he discovered in passing that Gollicker had also discarded the fishing pole and was leaping to tackle their enormous adversary. It was a brave, yet foolhardy, gesture. Showing a similar rapidity to when he had grabbed Tarbrush, the Negro caught the elderly man by the throat.

That was all Tarbrush saw. Continuing his involuntary

turn, he felt himself falling and realized he was plunging in the direction of Gollicker's buckboard. There was a popping crack behind him such as he had heard when a man who was being hanged was dropped through the trapdoor of the scaffold. Before he could look around, or do anything to halt his movements, his head struck the vehicle's rear wheel and, after a brief explosion of brilliantly colored flashes, everything went black.

In one respect Tarbush could account himself fortunate. Although unable to prevent the impact, he had already been losing momentum by the time he was going down. If he had not, he would almost certainly have suffered far worse damage than merely being stunned. As it was, in spite of losing consciousness, he suffered no serious or incapacitating injury.

About ten minutes elapsed without the young Negro stirring. Then, rolling on to his back, he eased himself slowly into a sitting position against the buckboard's wheel. Shaking his throbbing head caused it to clear, and with the return of cohesive thought, he began to remember what had taken place. The recollection drove him to lever his lanky frame erect, struggling to throw off the weakness and throbbing ache in his shoulders. Clinging to the side of the vehicle with his left arm, he dragged the Colt from his waistband in a shaking right hand and took stock of his surroundings.

Hearing and catching a slight movement beyond the buckboard from the corner of his eye, Tarbrush glanced in that direction. He found nothing to disturb him. It was only the aged draft horse grazing placidly. Turning his head slowly, for he still felt weak, he continued his examination. His mule was standing nearby, and in one respect, its presence was reassuring. While still somewhat restless and looking toward the backwater, whatever was holding its interest did not appear to be causing any undue alarm. There was no sign of the huge Negro, Tarbrush discovered. In fact, everything appeared to be as peaceful as when he had arrived.

Except—

"Oh, my Lord!" Tarbrush croaked, and shoving himself from the support of the buckboard, he went on uncertain legs toward the edge of the river.

Not until the young Negro arrived on the bank was he able to take in the full horror of the sight. From a distance, and because of the angle at which Gollicker's body was sprawled, it had not looked too bad. Up close Tarbrush found that the elderly man's head was inclined at an unnatural angle. Furthermore, the top of the skull was caved in so badly that there was little above the open and glassily staring eyes except shattered bone and ruptured flesh. Blood, already turning black as it congealed, matted the remaining white hair and mingled gruesomely with grayish brains that had oozed out onto the ground.

Nausea welled through Tarbrush. Letting out a low and disgusted moan he turned and vomited into the water. Having done so, although controlling his legs demanded a conscious effort, he walked slowly back to the buckboard. Tucking away the revolver he glanced quickly over his shoulder. Anger at the thought of how the kindly old man had been treated served to put badly needed strength back into his limbs. It also caused him to give thought to the situation.

The murderer had gone, but there was nothing to suggest he might be other than on foot. So he could not have traveled too far. That much was obvious to Tarbrush. Yet, while determined that Gollicker's death should not go unavenged, he realized that setting off alone was out of the question. Not only was he a stranger to this part of Texas, but the local law-enforcement officers must be informed of what had happened.

For a moment the young Negro considered loading the body onto the buckboard and taking it with him to Bannock's Ford. However, he soon saw the objections to adopting this line of action. To carry it out would slow him down and he wanted to set the wheels of retribution into motion with as little delay as possible. With that in mind he went to

54

and saddled the mule. Having done so, he mounted and, after a long look at the still shape by the backwater, rode from the clearing.

"Damn it to hell!" Toby Hooper muttered, not for the first time, glaring indignantly at the glow of lights from various premises in Bannock's Ford. "Where the hell's Silkie at?"

"Still in the town," Ivan Petrov answered, speaking casually although he, too, was growing worried and annoyed by their companion's continued absence.

"Yeah!" the young hardcase grumbled. "He's *still* in town and he's likely at one of the saloons, taking a drink while us two stay out here."

"It's possible," Petrov admitted, but—having no wish for Hooper to go in search of Roelich—went on, "If he is, he'll have a good reason for doing it."

Even while Silkie Roelich had been describing the course of action they were to take, the young hardcase had clearly disapproved. However, knowing that the other's temper was not of the best when crossed and being aware of his own limitations, he had confined himself to shifting restlessly in his saddle and scowling. After he and Petrov were left to their own devices and were concealed among the bushes on the fringe of the woodland, he had begun to grumble. His disgruntled state of mind had not improved when Roelich's failure to rejoin them became more protracted.

"Hell, we're just wasting our time here!" the young hardcase declared sullenly, kicking at a tuft of grass and changing the Henry rifle to the crook of his right arm. "If that son-of-a-bitching thing was coming this way, it'd've showed up afore now."

"Perhaps," Petrov replied, despite feeling that the other's summation had some justification. "But there is no telling what it will do, or where it will go."

"One thing's for certain sure," Hooper stated. "It can't go back where it come from 'less'n it can swim a hell of a way, or walk underwater."

"That's true," Petrov conceded, eager to keep the conversation going if it diverted the young hardcase's thoughts from dwelling upon the possibility that Roelich was relaxing at a saloon in the town. "Haiti is far from the United States."

"That's for sure," Hooper agreed, without having any idea as to the country in question's geographical location other than it was somewhere outside his homeland. "I'm damned if I know why you had to fetch the two of 'em all that way, though. You've picked the others up over here easy enough."

"Those two were already prepared," Petrov explained, but considered that the subject was one upon which he did not feel it advisable to elaborate, so decided to try to change it. "That is why they are so dangerous."

"You're not whistling Dixie they're dangerous!" Hooper exclaimed, his curiosity undiverted. "I saw those chains it busted. Are you *certain* that you can handle it?"

"I always have before," Petrov reminded the young man.

"Sure." Hooper grunted, looking dubious. "Only, things was different then. Anyways," he continued, indicating his rifle, "happen you-all can't, I for sure will. I'm not taking any chances with one of those sons of bitches."

"Shoot at the head if you have to use your weapon," Petrov advised, agreeing with the other's sentiments and doubts. "It's no use hitting anywhere else."

"I'll keep it in mind," Hooper promised, and glanced about him in an almost nervous fashion. "Damned if I know what anybody'd want with such things, though."

"They have their uses," Petrov answered, in a coldly forbidding tone which suggested that particular aspect of the conversation was not open for discussion.

"They *must* have," Hooper conceded, "happen somebody from that Haiti place's come out here to try'n'get them back."

"We don't know that anybody has!" Petrov snapped.

"Somebody's for sure been scouting the place," Hooper pointed out.

"People always get curious about anything they think is strange," Petrov countered, but in a way that seemed he was trying to reassure himself. "It may only be somebody from the town trying to find out what we are doing on the island and why we won't let them visit us. Or it could be a scout for some—how do you call them—bandidos who are wondering whether we'd be worth robbing."

"They'll be in for one hell of a surprise happen that's all they are and they manage to get out there," Hooper stated with a grin. "Happen we turn those damned things loose on 'em, they'll run like ole Santa Anna taking a greaser standoff after San Jacinto." However, another thought struck him and he swung his gaze to his companion, going on, "Hey! That nigger we met on the trail hasn't gone by yet!"

"That's right!" Petrov exclaimed. "He hasn't!"

"You don't reckon he could've heard what we was saying and knowed Silkie was lying about that grizzly being on the rampage in the woods and's gone hunting for it?"

"It's possible. If he wasn't what he told us and knows about it, he might have gone looking for it."

"Would he chance that, knowing what it is?"

"If he has been sent from Haiti, he would know how to control it," Petrov replied. "But Mr. Roelich was sure that he had told us the truth."

"Niggers make mighty convincing liars happen they've a mind to it," Hooper stated, coming as close as he dared to suggesting the older hired gun might have been deluded. "And he could've been over here for long enough to have learned to talk that way. There was something cagy about him, and he sure's hell didn't want to ride along with us. Could be he's gone hunting for it, knowing that his black hide'd keep him safe should he come across it."

"He might be wrong about that," Petrov contradicted. "It has been conditioned not to attack a colored person unless ordered to do so, but there's no telling what it might do— What's wrong?"

Toward the latter part of his explanation the thickset man

had become aware that he was no longer holding his companion's attention. Instead, Hooper had suddenly turned and was staring toward the town. At first Petrov wondered if he had seen or heard somebody approaching. A glance told the foreigner that such was not the case. In fact, he was unable to find anything that might have been the cause of the other's distraction. There had been a constant background of music and other sounds of people enjoying themselves from the distant buildings, but he could detect no change in its content or volume.

"I thought I heard some shots!" Hooper replied.

"What kind?" Petrov demanded, staring harder and straining his ears. "I don't hear any."

"It was only two or three at the most, from a handgun was being cut loose real fast," Hooper elaborated, then he stiffened and an alarmed expression came to his face. "Hell's fire! Maybe it's got by us and into town!"

"There's no more shooting," Petrov breathed, after listening for a few seconds. "Nor anything else out of the ordinary. If it had reached the town and been seen, there would have been much more noise."

"Could be it was Silkie's got it," Hooper suggested, then went on hopefully, "I'll go and find out for sure."

"No!" Petrov barked.

An angry grunt burst from the young hardcase at what was clearly an order rather than a request. Swinging around, he glared defiantly at the thickset foreigner. Their eyes seemed locked upon one another for several seconds, without either saying a word, in what was clearly a struggle for mastery.

Slowly, in spite of holding the Henry and knowing it was far more readily available than the Remington double derringer that Petrov always carried somewhere in his clothing, Hooper became conscious of a growing sensation of alarm. He had seen the other dealing with "those things" at the Island Mission and the sight had instilled a sense of superstitious awe, which he felt assailing him at that moment. Much as he would have liked to ignore the prohibition and carry out his suggestion, he was unable to do so. Instead, his only desire was to have those piercing eyes turn from him, and he accepted that there was only one way he could bring it about.

"Maybe you're right," Hooper said, trying to sound matter of fact, and dropping his gaze. "It was likely only some cowhand fooling with his gun. That damned thing just couldn't have gone by without us seeing it."

With that the young man resumed watching the woodland. If he had happened to glance down, he might have noticed something that flashed and scintillated in Petrov's left hand. At the first suggestion of opposition, holding Hooper's attention with his eyes, he had drawn an object from the left side pocket of his trousers. It was not a firearm, or anything else recognizable as a weapon; merely a small crystal globe in the shape of a diamond cut in the many-faceted style known as 'American Brilliant' and suspended on a slender piece of chain.

Several minutes dragged by in silence after Petrov had replaced the object in his pocket. He felt no desire to talk and doubted whether his companion had any inclination toward resuming their conversation. Neither of them heard further shooting, nor any other form of disturbance from the town.

Engrossed in their own thoughts the pair were caught unawares when a rider appeared from the woodland. They had selected their hiding place something over halfway between the river and the trail. Turning to gaze at the latter each reached the same conclusion.

"It's that damned nigger!" Hooper snarled, starting to move his rifle so that he would be able to use it, as he identified the fast-moving figure. "The way he's pushing that knobhead, he must've seen it!"

Before Petrov could reply, or even become aware of what he was doing, the young man managed to get the butt of the Henry to his shoulder. Sighting quickly, the delay in raising the weapon having allowed the galloping mule to carry its rider a fair way along the trail, he tugged at the trigger. The Henry cracked, but there was nothing to suggest its bullet had made a hit.

"Stop that!" Petrov commanded, glaring as his companion began to operate the Henry's reloading lever.

"He'll tell them about it in town!" Hooper protested, but refrained from firing a second time.

"Let him!" Petrov answered. "Mr. Roelich and the marshal will make sure that he isn't believed." Turning, he looked at the woods for a moment before continuing, "I wonder where it is now?"

CHAPTER SIX

THOSE HOLES COULD'VE BEEN IN YOU

"Take it easy, boy!" Blinky said with quiet, yet forceful, urgency as silence descended over the barroom of the Man on the Wall Saloon.

"Easy be damned!" Lonny Tapper spat back, barely aware of being the center of attention, as he glared furiously at the impassive-looking cause of his humiliation and wrath. "That white-faced son of a—!"

Thrown across the room from the direction of the bar, a hat landed on the table. In addition to knocking over a beer schooner, it served to bring the youngster's heated words to a halt before he could complete what—when used in such a tone—would have been an unforgivable insult. Taken equally unawares all the other participants in the game looked around to discover who was responsible for the interruption.

There was no difficulty in identifying the owner of the headdress. He was already walking forward. Tall, in his late thirties, lean as a steer raised in the greasewood country, he had neatly barbered black hair and a clean-shaven, ruggedly handsome face. His clothes were those of a working cowhand, but the Colt 1860 Army revolver resting against his right thigh was in a low-tied, fast-draw rig. There was an aura of purposeful self-assurance about him that suggested he was capable of backing up any play he started, even if it was —as now—intervening in somebody else's affairs. What was more, the deputy sheriff's star glinting on his calfskin vest indicated that he had a right to do so under the circumstances.

"Howdy, gents," the peace officer greeted in a low, laconic Texas drawl, halting with his right hand thumb-hooked in the gun belt not far from the Colt's walnut handle. "Seems like there's a difference of opinion here and you-all might need an outside help to settle the which 'n' what of it. Case you haven't noticed the badge and think I'm just billing in on personal doings 'cause I'm nosy, the name's Jervis Tragg. I'm a duly sworn 'n' appointed deputy sheriff of this here Kinney County." He paused, as if to let the pronouncement sink in, then continued without any noticeable change in his deceptively casual demeanor, "What's all the fuss?"

"I've been slickered—!" Tapper began.

"Apart from it being polite to start with the oldest gents, I allus like to hear the bystanders first," Tragg put in, once again causing the youngster to relapse into silence. In spite of his comment it was to Silkie Roelich that he directed his next remark. "Maybe *you'd* like to tell it, *mister?*"

"Doc theer pulled a mighty slick bluff," the hired gun obliged, guessing that the deputy—who he had heard was a mighty efficient lawman—had been keeping an eye on all that was taking place in the room and so it would be inadvisable to lie. However, he selected words that he hoped would help to achieve his purpose. "But the *youngster* here doesn't see it that way."

"You can bet your sweet life I don't!" Tapper yelped, finding that the reference to his youth was as rankling as his growing suspicion that he had merely fallen victim to a legitimate ploy by a more experienced and capable player. "Damn it! He hadn't done nothing like it afore—"

"Which's likely why he brought it off this time," Tragg said calmly, guessing how the situation had arisen from what he had seen while watching the game. Then he returned his gaze to the hired gun and he asked, "Are *you* satisfied with the play?"

"I wasn't in the pot, but I didn't *see* anything wrong," Roelich answered, hoping that the way he had phrased the second part would arouse Tapper's suspicions. "It was a bluff, nothing more than that."

"That how you-all saw it, gents?" Tragg inquired of the two older cowhands.

"Took me in for sure," Shuffles declared without hesitation. "I'd've sworn from the betting's Doc had a nine in the hole to fill his house."

"And me," Blinky seconded, sharing the deputy's desire to settle the matter peacefully. "Which, had I been in Lonny's shoes, I'd've played it the same way he did."

"Does *that* satisfy you-all?" Tragg asked, swinging his gaze to Tapper.

"Well, I—!" the youngster began, suddenly realizing that he was the subject of considerable attention from all sides of the room. "Aw, hell, I suppose so."

"Supposing isn't good enough," Tragg stated, wanting to leave no doubts that could come to a head later. "Way you jumped up, you was pretty damned sure something was wrong and all set to call down this gent here to prove it. Happen you still feel that way, it's better out in the open."

"Well—!" Tapper commenced hesitantly. Then, noticing the mocking smile being directed at him by Roelich, felt his courage was under question and did not want to let it seem that he had backed down. "All I can say is, his play changed mighty sudden."

"Which means you're not satisfied," Tragg drawled. "All right, both of you come with me."

Wondering what the peace officer was up to, Tapper obeyed. Equally puzzled, Doc Leroy rose and accompanied them, followed by the other players. Even as Roelich was deciding that he would learn nothing about the young man's ability as a gunfighter, he noticed that Tragg was not making for the front door; which would have been the case if the pair were being taken to the sheriff's office. Instead, he led the way across the room and halted about twenty feet away from the object that gave the saloon its name.

"Now, gents," the deputy said, indicating the man-sized and-shaped wooden target. "Seems to me like we've got us a situation here that could wind up with lead flying. So I'm kind of curious's to how it'll come out, should there be any betting on it, and being the sneaky kind's like to have an edge. What I want is for you-all to stand side by side here. Then I'll count to three and say, 'Fire,' and you both cut loose at good ole 'Marshal Wyatt Earp' there's fast as you can. Get set."

A sense of relief flooded through Tapper as he prepared to carry out the instructions. He had heard stories about the pallid-faced young man that were not calculated to arouse his enthusiasm over the prospect of a corpse-and-cartridge confrontation. Only the fact that the other's appearance had seemed to suggest they were wrong had led him into rashness. So he was not sorry for having been given an opportunity to find out whether the information was true or false without the risks involved in a real showdown.

Standing to one side and watching, Roelich was annoyed at himself for having failed to notice the deputy sheriff was in the room. However, he decided that the way in which the situation had developed would at least let him find out one thing he wanted to know, even if it did not solve his dilemma entirely.

"Get set!" Tragg ordered.

Like most youngsters in Texas Tapper had a well-developed interest in gunfighters and their activities. He had spent much time trying to emulate their exploits. Crouching in what he believed was the stance adopted by the best members of the fast-draw fraternity, he glanced to his left. Much to his surprise he found that his opponent had not adopted a similar posture. A sense of superiority began to rise as he concluded that he had been told tall tales where the other's abilities were concerned.

"One! Two! Three!" Tragg counted, spacing the numbers out evenly, and they were distinct in the silence that still lay over the room. "Fire!"

Even before the final word was spoken, Tapper grabbed the butt of his Colt. In spite of having that much advantage, he still had not cleared leather when his opponent acted upon the order.

The difference between the pair's style and capability was instantly apparent.

So swiftly and smoothly did Doc Leroy's right hand move that the ivory-handled Army Colt seemed to meet it in mid-air. Aimed at waist level and by instinctive alignment the weapon roared.

Hearing the crash of detonating black powder Tapper snapped his head around and did not complete his draw. Instead, he stared with fascination and awe as, deftly thumb-cocking the Colt's single-action mechanism, Doc Leroy fired two more shots so rapidly that the explosions almost merged into a single sound. Then, before the youngster's numbed brain could fully start to comprehend what had taken place, the revolver went back into its carefully contoured and shaped carrier. Still barely able to credit his eyes for having reported correctly, he turned them to the front. With a sensation as if an icy hand was running along his spine, he discovered that—swiftly as everything had happened—the "man on the wall" now had three .44 caliber holes so close together that the bullets that made them had all punctured his wooden heart.

"Hmph!" Tragg grunted, showing nothing of the fact that he, too, was impressed. He had heard that Doc Leroy was better than average with a Colt but had not appreciated just how much better. For all that, he forced himself to address Tapper in matter-of-fact tones. "Seeing's those holes could've been in you, I don't reckon's you'd be a good bet should it come to a showdown." Then he gave his left thigh a slap of mock exasperation as if a point had just struck him. "Hot damn! Everybody else's seen it, so they'll all know not to bet on you-all as well."

"Looks like you-all done slickered yourself, Jervis!" Blinky chortled, guessing what the deputy was doing and going along to help relieve the tension.

"Allus like to see somebody's does that," Shuffles went on, being just as discerning and eager to help. "Which I conclude *somebody* ought to put up the drinks."

"They're on me," Doc Leroy offered. "You'll join us, Jervis?"

"That's right neighborly of you-all, Doc," Tragg replied. "Only, way I've heard it, with you Wedge boys, the one who gets slickered pays. So it looks like it's up to me to set them up."

"I'd say me more than you, Jervis," Tapper put in, refusing to let it be thought a member of the Lazy Scissors could not follow the same rules as were practised by an outfit as well known and respected as the Wedge, for whom the pallid-faced young man rode. He saw his companions and the deputy grinning approval and continued with his effort to make amends for what he now saw to have been unsporting, incredibly foolhardy behavior. "Reckon I owe you an apology, Doc. You took me in fair and square."

"It's always been a good one to play, providing you don't pull it too often," the young man answered. "And make sure that *nobody* sees your hole card to find out what you've done."

"I'm sorry about that, Doc," Roelich said, wondering if the comment held an implied rebuke from him. He could not tell from the way in which it had been uttered. "The damned thing just slipped through my fingers."

"Nobody got hurt," Doc Leroy replied in the same neutral tones, but there was subtle difference as he went on, "Somebody said something about setting up a drink."

Conversation welled up around the room as its occupants watched the men returning to the table. It was obvious that, due to the deputy's timely intervention, there would be no more dramatic developments. So various interrupted activities were resumed.

"Hum, is that the time?" Doc Leroy inquired, glancing at

the wall clock as the drinks were being delivered. "I'm beat and could use some sleep, but I hate pulling out a winner." He sorted out the money in front of him, pocketing some of it, and went on, "Tell you what, this's near on all I've took. Happen you Lazy Scissors boys want to cover it one cut, winner take all, that way I won't feel so bad—And you, happen you're so minded, *Mr.* Roelich."

"I'm about holding my own," the hired gun answered, the slight emphasis on the honorific that had been used instead of "Silkie" suggesting the earlier comment had been a rebuke. "And, seeing that I've got to get back to the Island Mission tonight, I reckon I'll pull out after I've seen the way the cut goes."

"Come on." Blinky grinned, looking at his companions. "They do say luck beats skill all ways, so we'ns ought to whomp him good."

"I'm for it," Shuffles seconded, watching the slender young man gathering up the cards. "My daddy allus told me's it's better to be lucky'n good—which's how I's rich and famous's I am today."

"You-all stack them, Jervis," Doc Leroy requested, placing the deck on the table near the deputy. "Then cut them four ways and, happen nobody objects, we'll each take a heap and turn the top card over. High man takes the pot."

"That sounds fair enough to *me*," Tragg declared, with just a suggestion of a challenging glance at Roelich, and then doing as he was requested when nobody raised an objection. "There you are, gents. Who's going first?"

"I'll give her a whirl," Blinky stated, taking the right-hand pile and exposing the seven of hearts.

"Anyways," Shuffles drawled, showing the nine of diamonds from the second pile on the right. "I've licked you-all. Which don't mean sic 'em, afore anybody tells me."

"Blast it!" Tapper snorted, taking the five of spades from the left-hand heap.

"They do say that fortune favors the fair," Doc Leroy drawled, extending an obvious empty hand and flipping over—as far as was discernible—the uppermost card from the remaining stack. "Which I should've remembered my hair's brown not fair."

"Whoooe, Doc!" Tapper whooped, his natural good humor entirely restored at the sight of the—to him in particular—fateful deuce of diamonds in the other's slender right hand. "It's sure's hell wasn't lucky for you-all this time."

"It wasn't *lucky* last time," Doc Leroy corrected just as cheerfully, but his eyes went briefly to Roelich before he ended, "And I yield to our senior player. Luck does lick skill in the end."

While the rest of the group chuckled, the hired gun felt distinctly uneasy. Without betraying his suspicions he sensed that the young man had deduced what he was hoping to achieve. Furthermore, his every instinct told him that —although he had seen nothing amiss—the result of the cutting had not been entirely unexpected where Doc Leroy was concerned. Nor had a pure coincidence selected that particular card to reappear. However, having been granted the demonstration he desired, he was disinclined to make his sentiments in public. So, having said his good-byes, he left the building. Instead of mounting his horse and riding away he walked along until he could look inside through a window.

"Oh, well," Doc Leroy drawled, shortly after the hired gun had taken his departure. "I reckon I'll drift along and get me some sleep."

"It's time I was making the rounds, come to that," Tragg remarked. "Otherwise the good taxpaying folks of this fair city might start thinking I'm not earning my pay. So I'll drift along with you-all, Doc, happen you've no objections."

"It could ruin my standing socially," the young man answered, "but I've never had any and I'll not miss it."

Accompanying the deputy from the saloon Doc paused just outside the doors and looked around. By that time Roelich had withdrawn to the darkness of an alley at the other side of the street and could not be seen.

"You-all too tired to feel like talking a mite?" Tragg inquired, but there was something in his attitude that warned he would prefer that the answer was not in the negative.

"Thought you might say that," Doc admitted. "Where'll we go?"

"Along to the jailhouse," Tragg suggested. "The sheriff's got an office there and, happen I know the town clown, neither him nor any of his deputies'll be around."

"That's no way to talk about a brother officer of the law." Doc Leroy grinned, although the little he had seen of Marshal Arthur Gormley had not given him a higher opinion than that of the deputy.

"Day he gets to be *my* brother," Tragg sniffed, "that's when I turn in my badge."

Neither of the men discussed anything of importance during the short stroll to the sturdily built adobe building that served as a combined jail and offices for both municipal and county law-enforcement departments. Entering the unlocked front door they found that Tragg's summation had been correct and there was nobody else present. The deputy led the way into the office at the right side front of the structure, which was assigned to the county sheriff and his men. A lantern hung glowing from its hook on the ceiling, showing it to be much the same as might be expected in a similar room anywhere in the West.

"Grab a chair," Tragg offered, sitting behind the old desk and hooking up a long leg so his boot added to the numerous other scuff marks on its top. "How'd you pull off that cut?"

"Pull?" Doc Leroy countered, oozing innocence.

"Dirk Damon from Lampasas County's an old friend of mine," the deputy stated amiably. "He's told me how Joe Brambile taught you to handle a deck of cards. What'd you do, palm that deuce?"

"Would I do that and lose most all I'd won?" the young man challenged, still innocently, despite realizing that the deputy must be trustworthy if the sheriff of Lampasas

County—an old family friend—had given so much information.

"You might, seeing's how doing it would make sure that there wasn't any hard feelings left behind," Tragg replied. "Biggin down to the livery barn said you was asking about there being any hired guns hereabouts. Would that account for the one who was in the game sitting in?"

Having followed the two men Roelich had arrived at the front of the jailhouse undetected. He had just taken up a position, leaning against the wall close to the window of the sheriff's office—but out of its occupants' sight—when the deputy asked the question and he waited eagerly for the reply.

"It might have," Doc Leroy admitted. "I should've figured that jasper at the barn was a blabbermouth."

"Not too much," Tragg corrected. "He doesn't go spouting off promiscuous. He only told me because he allowed I'd likely to know what to do better'n good ole Marshal Gormley, who he'd already let in on it. What'd you-all have in mind?"

"I was a mite suspicious when that hombre sat in," the young man explained. "The game wasn't high enough for him to want to take cards just to pass the time. Got even more sure when, unless I'm doing him an injustice, he deliberately let young Tapper see my hole card."

"Why'd he do that?" Tragg inquired, although he could guess.

"Either he wanted to find out how good I am with a gun, or hoped Tapper and his amigos would gang up and take me out."

"Would he have any reason to want to know, or to have you took out?"

"None that I can think of. To the best of my knowledge I've never set eyes on him before tonight. Who is he?"

"Goes by the name of Silkie Roelich," Tragg replied. "He's boss gun for that Professor Morbeus who's up on the Island Mission."

` "Boss gun, huh?" Doc Leroy repeated, and went on half to himself, "Then Hayden Lindrick's not there. *He* wouldn't be riding seconds to anybody."

"Hayden Lindrick," Tragg said, frowning a little. "I've never heard anything of him since . . ."

"Or me," the young man stated, guessing why the deputy's words had trailed off in such an embarrassed fashion.

Anybody who was a friend of Dirk Damon would know why Doc Leroy had been asking about the possibility of hired guns in the vicinity of the town. Hayden Paul Lindrick had, as far as was known, been responsible for the murder of his parents. The circumstances had also ruined his chance of following in his father's footsteps as a qualified doctor.* Instead, he had become a cowhand and joined Stone Hart's Wedge, an outfit that owned neither land nor cattle, but took trail herds on contract for ranchers who did not wish to do so on their own account.

"I can't say's I've ever met Lindrick, although I've seen his description on the wanted dodgers Dirk put out," Tragg remarked. "And, if he's at the Mission, he's never come into town while I was here. Course, I don't stay here all the time. Once a month or so the sheriff sends me along to make sure nobody's snuck off the jailhouse from under Gormley's nose."

"Like I said," Doc answered. "In the old days he would only take on as boss gun. But he could by lying low out there and letting Roelich allow that he's the boss. That dodger Dirk sent out's still open."

"And he's likely heard that you're still after him," Tragg pointed out.

"I don't reckon that'd scare him," Doc replied. "He was always a regular snake with those two fancy li'l Colts he carried. But if he is out there, Roelich could've figured to do him a good turn by getting me made wolf bait."

* Told in Doc LEROY, M.D.—J.T.E.

"It might be," Tragg conceded.

"Best place to find out for sure'd be at the Mission," Doc commented.

Before Roelich could learn how the deputy reacted to the cowhand's suggestion, a rifle cracked in the distance. A low curse burst from him, for it had originated from the area in which he had left his companions. Swinging around and staring in that direction he was unable to see anything to explain why the weapon had been discharged. Nor, having moved away from the window, was he able to hear what was being said in the office. However, after several seconds had elapsed without any more shooting, he was on the point of resuming his interrupted eavesdropping when the sound of rapidly approaching hooves reached his ears.

Deciding that he should go and find out who the rider might be, Roelich started to move quietly across the sidewalk. Stepping onto the street he noticed a shape in the shadows of an alley at the other side. It was moving away into the deeper blackness, but a door farther along was opened. The glow of light that was thrown out illuminated the slender figure of a woman. Although she was walking away from him and did not look back, he realized that it was the same person who had attracted his attention while he was talking to the marshal.

CHAPTER SEVEN

SOMETHING, OR *SOMEBODY?*

For a moment Silkie Roelich thought of following the woman and trying to find out if she was taking an interest in his affairs, or whether the fact that he had seen her twice in similar circumstances was no more than a harmless coincidence. Common sense warned him against adopting such a line of action. In the event that only chance was involved, she might misinterpret his intentions and cause an undesirable disturbance. On the other hand, if she should be watching him for some reason, she would know that she had aroused his suspicions and take greater care to avoid him.

Furthermore, the hired gun realized that there was another matter demanding his attention. Listening to the hoofbeats coming nearer and at an undiminished speed, he realized that investigating the reason for such haste could under the circumstances be of greater importance. If the rider should be either Ivan Petrov or Toby Hooper, he wanted to discover what was bringing whichever it was to town in a manner calculated to attract unwanted attention. Or, should it turn out that a chance passing rider had been fired upon by the latter, he felt that it would be advisable for him to be close by when the matter was reported to the local peace officers. In that way he would be able to judge what action to take and, providing that Marshal Arthur Gormley and not Deputy Sheriff Jervis Tragg took charge, he could ensure that everything was handled in an advantageous fashion.

A quick glance into the alley informed Roelich that the

woman had kept walking and was no longer in view. So he threw a quick glance at the jailhouse to find out if there was any cause for concern in that direction. As the deputy was still sitting at the desk in conversation with Doc Leroy, it was obvious that they had not yet heard the approaching rider. So there was a chance that, as was desirable from his point of view, Gormley would be the first peace officer to put in an appearance.

Striding swiftly along the street Roelich was soon able to identify the rider as the young Negro to whom he and his companions had spoken on the trail. There were two possible reasons for the big brown mule being pushed along at a full gallop. Either its owner merely wanted to reach the safety of the town after having been shot at by Hooper, or he had seen the thing that had escaped from the Island Mission. The hired gun hoped that it was the former.

Much to Roelich's annoyance the marshal did not put in an appearance. So, as the Negro continued to ride at an unabated pace, on reaching the street he turned and hurried into an unlit alley. From there he watched the rider go by without exposing himself to the risk of being seen. Brief though his glimpse of the other's face was in passing, its expression was such that he felt sure that the haste was resulting from the latter alternative rather than a desire to avoid further bullets. Silently cursing Hooper for having fired, or—if it was necessary—missing, and Gormley's failure to show up when needed, he remained in his place of concealment to await the next developments.

Although Tarbrush had never been to Bannock's Ford, he had seen sufficient during his hurried approach to guess where the local peace officers were to be located. So, paying no attention to the people who stared at him as he rushed by, he kept the mule running along the street until he saw what could only be the jailhouse. Bringing the hard-pushed animal to a rump-sliding halt before the building, he almost tumbled from the saddle. Allowing the reins to slip out of his grasp, swaying on his feet as a result of his exertions, he hurried toward the front door. It was jerked open while he was crossing the sidewalk and he saw two men, one wearing a deputy sheriff's badge, in front of him.

"What's up?" Jervis Tragg demanded, having heard the mule during the final stages of its dash along the street and come from the sheriff's office to investigate.

"Th-there's b-been m-murder d-done!" Tarbrush gasped and stumbled.

Catching the Negro by the arms Doc Leroy and Tragg helped him into the room from which they had come. The deputy had been telling the cowhand about the peculiar state of affairs where the Island Mission was concerned, but each put the subject from his mind. Seating Tarbrush at the desk Tragg went to and unlocked the office's small safe.

"He'll feel better after he's taken a snort of this," the deputy announced, lifting out a bottle of whiskey and a glass. "Do you fancy one, Doc?"

"Not right now, *gracias,*" the cowhand replied, studying the Negro and guessing that more than the effects of what had clearly been a long, hard ride was responsible for his exhausted condition. "Do you want me to go?"

"Stay on, happen you've nothing special to do," Tragg offered, knowing how the other had acquired his nickname. "He doesn't look in any too good shape, and seeing's how old Doctor Gollicker's—"

"D-doctor!" Tarbrush put in with an agonized croak. "It—he—it—!"

"Here, you-all drink this," Tragg ordered, having poured a good four fingers of the liquor into the glass. "Then you'll be able to tell us."

"It's the doctor's's been killed," Tarbrush began, feeling slightly better and more composed after having taken the deputy's advice.

"Who did it?" Tragg demanded, but in a gentle tone.

"The good Lord, or more likely the devil, only knows who he was," Tarbrush answered. His hand shook as he put

75

down the empty glass, but he had his thoughts in order once more. "I've never seen anybody like him afore and ain't wanting to again."

"Who?" Tragg prompted patiently, as the memory of the murderer's awesome appearance brought the young Negro's words to a halt.

"This feller's come busting out of the bushes back there," Tarbrush replied, and a shudder shook him. "Lordy lord! That was the biggest, ugliest, most evil-looking cuss I've ever come across."

Forcing himself to take control of his emotions, Tarbrush told of the incident at the backwater on the Rio Grande. Starting with his first sight of Doctor Gollicker he watched his two-man audience in hope of learning how they were receiving his story. He noticed that the deputy gave a slight nod of agreement when he mentioned how he had been invited to participate. It was clear that his host's love of fishing was well known, but he was unsuccessful in determining whether the rest of his story was striking the peace officer as equally acceptable. In fact, when he was describing the assailant, he saw Tragg exchange glances with the other occupant of the office.

"What did you say your name was?" the deputy asked, when the explanation came to an end.

"I'd sure hate to have to tell you-all how my folks had me baptized," the young Negro declared truthfully, having no love for the grandiloquent names he had been given at his christening. "What I answer to best is Tarbrush."

"Are you-all the feller's rode Nighthawk for Dusty Fog when he took that OD Connected herd to Dodge City against Wyatt Earp's Injun-sign?" Doc Leroy inquired.

"I rode for Cap'n Fog, all right," Tarbrush confirmed. "Only, he was trail boss for Ben Holland's Rocking H on that drive."*

"My mistake," Doc drawled.

* Told in TRAIL BOSS.—J.T.E.

Nothing in the pallid-faced cowhand's demeanor suggested that the error had been other than accidental. Yet, considering certain facts with which he was acquainted, Tarbrush considered he had been tested and passed.

"You say this here big hombre jumped you for no cause," Tragg remarked, almost as if making no more than casual conversation. "Then, having caught hold of you-all, he just heaved you to one side; but that he killed Doctor Gollicker."

"That's how it happened," Tarbrush stated. "I know there's not many colored folks live hereabouts, but you'd surely known one who looked like he did."

"I would," Tragg conceded. "Only, I don't."

"Look here!" Tarbrush said, starting to rise. "I've told you-all the truth—"

"I've never thought otherwise," the deputy said calmly. "Anybody who wasn't't'd've come up with a story a damned sight more likely than yours." His gaze flickered to the cowhand and he went on, "Are you too tired to come out there with me, Doc?"

"I reckon I could stay awake for a while yet," the cowhand replied.

"*Bueno,*" the deputy said, realizing that—in spite of his ambition to become a qualified doctor having been curtailed—the other possessed a medical knowledge that could be of help in the forthcoming investigation. "If you'll get a hoss for this gent, have Biggin saddle mine up and fetch your'n, we'll go out and bring back the body."

"I'll do that," Doc assented. "Can anybody handle that old mule, Tarbrush?"

"Just so long's they know what they're doing and do it easy," the Negro replied, "specially when he's been run's hard's I've just now run him."

"Then I'll see he's tended to for you," Doc promised.

At that moment the door of the office was thrown open and the town marshal strode in. His face was even more flushed than usual, but a certain unsteadiness in his gait suggested that the increased color did not entirely stem from his having hurried while coming to the jailhouse.

"What's up, Jervis?" Gormley demanded, and the slightly slurred timbre of the words added strength to the supposition that he had been drinking. "I saw the nigger here coming through town like a bat out of hell."

"He was hurrying to report a crime, *Marshal,*" the deputy replied, controlling his distaste. Like every decent southron he never employed the word *nigger*—particularly in the presence of a colored person—or cared to hear it used. "It's out of town, so I'll have to tend to it."

"Yeah, it's in your bailiwick, not mine," Gormley replied, his cheeks becoming even more suffused. Despite the even tone Jervis Tragg's use of the honorific was anything but complimentary and he guessed the dislike went beyond the rivalry that often existed between municipal and county peace officers where jurisdiction matters were involved. "If you want any help—"

"I'll let you know," the deputy promised, still speaking blandly, but the subtle difference in his attitude was plain as he addressed the Negro. "Are you-all up to riding yet, *mister?*"

"Are you arresting him?" Gormley asked, before Tarbrush could answer.

"Should I be?" Tragg inquired, but there was a hint of challenge in his words.

"No," Gormley confessed, but his response did not come immediately. It almost seemed to the deputy that he had been trying to think of a reason that would justify an affirmative answer. "I can't seen any reason why you should."

As Tarbrush had not mentioned his meeting with Roelich's party, the story he had been told about the rampaging grizzly bear, or being shot at on his way into town, Tragg did not draw any significance from the marshal's questions. Instead, he put them down to having been inspired by nothing more than ignorant racial prejudice.

"We'll go down and get the horses from the livery barn,"

the deputy informed the young Negro, coming to his feet. "I'll let you know what happens, Marshal."

"Sure," Gormley grunted, sounding almost disinterested. Then, in what was plainly an afterthought, he went on, "What'd you say he came here for?"

"To tell me that Doctor Gollicker's been murdered," Tragg replied, seeing nothing unusual in the fact that such a question had not occurred to Gormley earlier.

"M-murdered?" the marshal yelped, shock sobering him up. "Who did it?"

"That's what we're going to see if we can find out," Tragg answered, being disinclined to become involved in a lengthy discussion over what the Negro had told him. "We'd best be moving, mister."

"Sure, Sheriff," Tarbrush agreed, not caring for the baleful way in which the other peace officer was glowering at him. "I'm ready."

For his part Gormley was unable to decide what to do next. He had taken rather more drinks than was advisable during his vigil at the Ranchero Saloon. So he had neither heard Hooper's rifle shot nor paid any attention when Tarbrush galloped by. It was not until Roelich had appeared and signaled for him to come outside that he discovered something was amiss. On joining the hired gun he had been given only a little information and not much guidance, being told to find out why the Negro had arrived in such a hurry and to cast doubts on any references that might be made to the thing that had escaped from the Island Mission. Having delivered his instructions, Roelich had mounted with the announced intention of rejoining his companions.

Leaving the marshal, after locking the bottle of whiskey away in the safe, Tragg escorted Tarbrush from the jailhouse. As they walked to the livery barn, where Doc had already taken the leg-weary mule, the deputy asked to have the description of the murderer repeated. While the repetition did little to make the story sound more credible, Tragg still considered that he was being told the truth. Yet he knew a man of such an unpleasantly unusual appearance could hardly have lived locally, even in a large community of colored people—which Bannock's Ford did not have—without being at least the subject of comment.

On their arrival Tragg and Tarbrush found that Doc Leroy had wasted no time. He was already saddling his big black gelding, while Biggin was preparing the deputy's powerful dun and a youngster made one of the establishment's mounts ready for use by the Negro. It was also apparent from the ostler's attitude that the cowhand had given only the minimum of information respecting their need for the animals.

"You got trouble, Jervis?" asked the plump, balding, and middle-aged owner of the barn, without interrupting his work.

"Some," Tragg admitted vaguely, and continued in a casual-sounding fashion, "Seen anything of Doctor Gollicker?"

"Not since early on," Biggin replied, finding nothing out of the ordinary in the question as the matter claiming the peace officer's attention might require the services of a medical man. "But don't ask me where he's at now. He took off in his buckboard with his fishing gear in it, allowing he'd been hard at it recently and reckoned he deserved a rest."

"He's been sneaking off 'n' baiting that big ole backwater upstream a ways," the youngster put in. "So that's where you-all'll likely find him."

"Gracias," Tragg said. "Has anybody else been around asking after him?"

"Not here," Biggin stated, and his assistant gave a nod of confirmation. "Folks know better'n go bothering him few times he does set his mind on taking off for a spell of fishing."

While the conversation had been taking place, the work of saddling was continued. When they were ready, the three men led the horses outside and mounted. Tragg asked Biggin to take care of Tarbrush's mule and, on being assured that this would be done, led the way out of town.

Track Down And Capture Exciting Western Adventure!

WANTED!

LOUIS L'AMOUR
COLLECTION!

REWARD OFFERED

Mail your "WANTED"
poster today. (see inside)

Make your
"wanted" claim
and receive your
rightful reward!

• A free authentic Louis
L'Amour calendar!

• A free preview of the
bestselling SACKETT

And much more…

Track down and capture exciting western adventure from one of America's foremost novelists!

• It's free! • No obligation! • Exclusive value!

"I sure hope whoever's hunting along the woods's a mite more careful," the young Negro commented, recollecting his narrow escape during the journey in, although he failed to connect it with the three men he had encountered earlier. "He was like to blow my head off as we come by."

"Some damned fools can't be trusted with guns," Tragg replied, but he was thinking about another matter. He had had something at the back of his mind ever since he and Doc were discussing the incident at the Man on the Wall Saloon. Now that his attention had been diverted from it for a time, the answer came to him. "Mind what I was saying about Biggin not talking promiscuous?"

"Why, sure," answered the cowhand, to whom the words had been directed, beginning to have an inkling of what the deputy was thinking. "He for sure didn't mention there being hired guns out to the Island Mission when I was asking."

"Nope," Tragg drawled. "And he wouldn't have told Roelich about you—"

"Did you-all say 'Roelich,' Sheriff?" Tarbrush interrupted.

"Sure," Tragg confirmed. "Why?"

"I met up with him on the trail into town afore I ran across the doctor," Tarbrush explained. "He told me's how there was a right mean ole grizzly bear on the rampage hereabouts."

"If there is," Tragg said, sounding puzzled, "nobody's told me about it."

"The doctor didn't mention it neither," Tarbrush went on. "But, way Roelich and the young feller was toting their rifles on their arms and acting, they was for sure looking for *something.*"

"Which young feller?" asked the deputy.

"Tall, young, but with the look of a hired gun," Tarbrush replied. "Name of Hooper, or some such."

"If it's Hooper, he's one of the Island crowd," Tragg declared.

"You said there was two with him," Doc remarked, anticipating the question that the peace officer was on the point of asking. "Who was the other one?"

"A dude," Tarbrush supplied. "Talked mighty funny and had real scary eyes."

"Would he be about medium height, thickset, and look like he could have a mite of Chinese blood?" Tragg asked and, on receiving a nod of agreement, continued, "That'd be Petrov, or some such name. He's a kind of ramrod for that professor out to the Mission. But neither him nor Hooper were around's I saw."

"Or me," Doc admitted. "Could word've got to that Mission place that I was in town and asking about hired guns, so they came to find out why?"

"There'd've been time," Tragg estimated. "And I'd think that's what it was, 'cepting for two things."

"Who sent the word to them," Doc suggested, "and why did they lie about the grizzly to Tarbrush?"

"Them's the two," Tragg confirmed. "And I can't think up an answer to either. Was those three hombres cowhands, I'd say they was only trying to throw a scare into you as a joke, Tarbrush. But none of them're the funning kind."

"That jasper with the scary eyes for sure ain't," the Negro stated. "And, way they was talking without knowing I could hear 'em, they was on the lookout for something *real* dangerous and didn't want me to see it."

"Something, or *somebody?*" Doc said quietly.

"How's that?" Tragg inquired.

"That feller's killed the doctor had to come from someplace and he'd be mighty noticeable wherever it is," Doc explained. "Only way he wouldn't get talked about was if he could be kept out of folks' sight, and from what you've told me, that could be done at the Island Mission."

"It could," the deputy conceded. "Only, why the hell would anybody want to keep a jasper like that around?"

"Wouldn't want to sound all pushy, or like I'm trying to tell you-all your work, Sheriff," Tarbrush commented. "But, you being the law 'n' all, mightn't it be a good notion to go to that place 'n' ask?"

"Doing that isn't so easy's it sounds," Tragg answered.

"There *has* to be a way," Doc declared, remembering the deputy's explanation when he had made a similar suggestion in the sheriff's office. It had been interrupted by the young Negro's arrival before they could carry out an extended discussion.

"We'll try to think of one, happen anything points to that jasper having come from there," Tragg promised, scanning the woods on either side of the trail. "Right now, though, happen he's still around, I'd's soon get to know it *afore* he gets close enough to jump us."

Accepting the wisdom of the deputy's comment the other two lapsed into silence. However, as had happened while Tarbrush was conducting his earlier precautionary survey, they reached the clearing without having seen or heard anything to suggest that the murderer still lurked in the vicinity.

"What the hell?" Tarbrush exclaimed, gazing around the open ground in amazement.

There was good cause for the young Negro's comment. With one *very* important exception, everything was exactly the same as he had left it. The aged horse still grazed patiently near the buckboard. Fishing poles, picnic basket, and bait bucket were on the edge of the backwater.

But the body of Doctor Gollicker was missing!

CHAPTER EIGHT

MAYBE THEY'LL WANT TO LYNCH HIM

"What I don't see is why you left all Gollicker's gear there when you toted off his body to hide it," Marshal Arthur Gormley protested, looking nervously at the two men who had summoned him secretly from the jailhouse and, having taken him to a deserted old building on the upstream side of the town, were telling him things he would rather not have heard.

"Because handling it that way gives you-all a reason to have that skinny nigger tossed in jail when they come back, even if Tragg doesn't do it without needing your advice," Silkie Roelich explained, employing the kind of manner people frequently adopt when addressing a far from intelligent child. "And in jail's where we want the son of a bitch."

"Then why not've left everything—!" the peace officer began, wishing that Ivan Petrov would stop watching him in such an unnerving fashion.

"Because Jervis Tragg's nobody's fool is why," the hired gun replied, a note of impatience creeping into his voice. "You can bet that that nigger's told him more than just what happened to Gollicker. He'll have mentioned meeting us on the trail and, most likely, even about me allowing there was a grizzly on the rampage along the river. So we don't want Tragg to see the body."

"Why?" Gormley asked, before he could stop himself.

"You wouldn't need to ask that, if you'd seen it," Roelich growled, and although he did not continue with, *Or maybe* you *would,* the words were implied by his tone. "The way the skull was caved in, it looked like it'd've took a grizzly at least to do it. A feller's skinny as that nigger couldn't have done it. So, unlikely as his story might sound, Tragg'd've been willing to reckon that he could have been telling the truth. As it is now, Gollicker's disappeared and there's enough blood around to show he didn't go peaceable or healthy. When they come back, even if Tragg hasn't already got the notion, you'll be able to say that the nigger has to be held until it's found out for sure what's happened—especially seeing's how the words got around about Gollicker being killed."

"It can't've—!" Gormley commenced hurriedly, worried by the possibility that he would be blamed for the information having been circulated.

"Yes, it can," Roelich corrected, and his impatience was becoming increasingly apparent. "I've got Hooper and a couple more hombres out spreading it. Folks hereabouts liked good old Gollicker. They'll not take it kind when they hear's he's been done to death and his body can't be found, specially when it gets around that a nigger's knows more'n he should about it's being held at the jailhouse. They're going to be riled, Marshal. Maybe they'll want to lynch him."

"Lynch him!" Gormley repeated, staring at the hired gun, and his voice took on a worried timbre as he continued, "Tragg'll figure on stopping them if they try it."

Remembering that law enforcement at state level was now carried out by the Texas Rangers, a far more capable and efficient body than the generally corrupt and incompetent state police they had supplanted at the end of Reconstruction, the peace officer was liking what he was hearing less and less by the second. There was no chance of preventing the news from spreading if Jervis Tragg should be killed while trying to prevent a lynching. Gormley was all too aware that a number of his own activities would not bear scrutiny and were almost certain to be brought to light in the investigation of the incident. However, he received little comfort from his companions.

"That's what us law-abiding and upright citizens of Kinney County pay him to do, for shame," Roelich answered, studying the marshal's obvious nervousness sardonically. "And, seeing's how we're paying *you-all* to do the same, you'll be right there to help him keep the peace."

"He's likely to have more than just me!" Gormley warned, alarmed by the possibility that he might be expected to pave the way for the lynch mob by removing the deputy. "Like I told you, Leroy didn't come here to find out about the Mission, but he'll back up Tragg if it comes to trouble."

Having learned the reason for the pallid-faced and chain-lightning-fast young man's visit to Bannock's Ford while he was drinking at the Ranchero Saloon, the marshal had passed on his findings as he was accompanying Roelich and Petrov to the house from which they were keeping an eye on the trail. Although the hired gun had heard of the range war in which Doc's parents were killed, he had forgotten the details. Nor, as he spent little time in the company of cowhands, had he heard of Doc's various accomplishments.

"Be a good man to have at your side, I'd say," Roelich drawled. "Specially when you're fixing to stop the lynch mob."

"It might not come to *that*," Gormley growled, annoyed by the hired gun's mocking attitude and feeling sure that he had overlooked one point in whatever he was planning. "Even without Leroy, Tragg's known hereabouts's a man it don't pay to fuss with. Could be nobody'll be willing to go up against him."

"Could be," Roelich conceded dryly, deciding that time was too short for him to continue indulging in the baiting of the surly peace officer. "But there's always *one* in every crowd who just won't give up when his mind's set on doing something."

"Hey, Deputy!" called one of the men who had emerged and gathered on the sidewalk outside the Ranchero Saloon, "Is that there the nigger's done poor old Doctor Gollicker to death?"

"Happen it is," another of the crowd went on, in tones of similar partly drunken truculence. "We'n's can save you-all needing to trouble any more with him."

Listening to the words and observing the menacing demeanor of the men from his place on the driving seat of the doctor's buckboard, Tarbrush glanced from left to right. Finding that his companions were coming to a stop, he signaled for the old horse to do the same. Even though he noticed that the deputy was positioned between him and the crowd, he began to feel uneasy. Although he had been treated well and fairly by the majority of white people with whom he had come into contact, he knew that the hatreds and bitterness created during the Reconstruction period had neither been forgiven nor forgotten. So he was aware that his life might be in grave danger.

After finding out that the corpse had disappeared, Tarbrush had been unsuccessful in determining what Jervis Tragg and Doc Leroy were thinking. He had appreciated how unlikely, fantastic even, his description of the events must have sounded. For all that, up to their arrival at the clearing, he had been convinced that the two white men were inclined to believe him.

Faced with the inexplicable circumstances and watching the deputy and the cowhand as they studied their surroundings, the young Negro had felt relieved that it was they and not the town marshal who had accompanied him. Even after such a short acquaintance he was already impressed by their acumen and felt sure that they could come up with a solution to the mystery. While they had failed to justify his confidence, their findings were not completely negative. There had been sufficient signs, such as the quantity of blood and other debris on the ground, to suggest that a violent death had occurred. Unfortunately, particularly in the inadequate illumination from the moon, the nature of the terrain did not allow the reading of tracks. Nor had their probing of the backwater to the limits of the fishing poles located the missing body. However, for all that their efforts had proved abortive, he could not claim they had skimped in their efforts to verify his story. In fact, they had devoted over an hour to their futile search for evidence that would corroborate—or disprove—it.

Apart from asking Tarbrush to hitch the horse to the buckboard and drive it, Tragg had said little. Nor had Doc been in any more of a communicative mood during the journey back to town. Oppressed by their silence the young Negro had decided against trying to discover what their sentiments might be. Now, from all appearances, he would very soon find out in no uncertain fashion.

"I'm not exactly sure what you gents're talking about," Tragg declared, with an air of complete calm, but thumb-hooking his right hand in his gun belt close to the holstered revolver in a way that did not pass unnoticed by the crowd.

"Maybe Jem here didn't put it plain enough for you-all, *deputy,*" the first speaker stated, but making sure that he remained among his companions instead of moving in front as befitted their self-appointed representative. "If that damned nigger's killed good ole Doctor Gollicker, we're all of a mind's he should stretch rope for it."

"You-all won't get any argument from me on *that,*" Tragg drawled, still slouching on his saddle in a deceptively casual fashion—which fooled nobody, nor was intended to—and alert to the reactions of his audience. "Fact being, *if* he's killed *anybody* at all, he should be took for *trial* in front of a *judge* and *jury;* then, *after* it's been *proved,* get hanged. Only, so far's I know, he's done *nothing* wrong."

"We'n's've heard different!" the first speaker declared, although he and every one of his cronies were aware of the emphasis placed by the deputy upon certain significant words in the statement.

There was a general—if muted—mumble of concurrence, but none of those who were responsible for it offered to move closer to the trio on the street.

"Happen you-all're certain *sure* that what you've heard is true," Tragg said, yet with a note of warning underlying the almost gentle-sounding words, "I'll let you have him right now." Ignoring the sound of the young Negro sucking in a deep and worried breath, he went on in an even grimmer tone, "Only, *you'd* better be right. Tarbrush here rides for the OD Connected—and I reckon's you-all know how Cap'n Fog feels about standing by Ole Devil Hardin's hired hands?"

Studying the crowd with eyes of one who was possessed of a very sound understanding where human nature was concerned, Doc Leroy realized that the deputy was handling the situation in a masterly fashion. The men on the sidewalk belonged to the worst elements of Texas's noncriminal society. Similar loafers could be found in almost every community, especially one of such rapid growth and potential wealth as Bannock's Ford. They were ready to do anything except work harder than was absolutely necessary and, provided that it did not entail too many risks, were willing participants should there be any mischief brewing. As yet none of them had drunk enough to have acquired a spurious courage. Nor was their intake of liquor too great for them to be able to comprehend the implications behind the deputy's comment.

With the latter factor in mind the cowhand could see Jervis Tragg's audience were impressed by the suggestion that Tarbrush was a member of General Jackson Baines "Ole Devil" Hardin's great OD Connected ranch. It was an outfit with a well-deserved reputation for standing by and supporting its employees in times of trouble. Furthermore, even without the very efficient assistance upon which he could call, its *segundo*—Captain Dustine Edward Marsden "Dusty" Fog, C.S.A. —was exceptionally capable of expressing resentment of any mistreatment to those who rode for his brand.

"Dusty Fog's not in town," the spokesman pointed out, but there was a most satisfactory uncertainty in his tone.

"He's not that far off either," Tragg countered, and continued with such sincerity that he might have been speaking the truth. "Fact being, he sent his Nighthawk here on ahead with a letter to the customs officers saying there'll be an OD Connected herd coming over the river either tomorrow or the next day."

There was an uneasy muttering from the would-be lynch mob. That the *segundo* of the OD Connected would take the trouble to notify the appropriate authorities of his intention to bring a herd into the United States and incur the customs duty that was imposed came as no surprise. Furthermore, he would in all probability send the message by one of the more menial and easily spared hands such as the Nighthawk.

"That don't mean's he didn't—" the spokesman commenced, having been paid to stir up his companions and sensing their indecision.

"Maybe not," Doc drawled, moving his horse forward until it was plain for every member of the crowd to see he had an uninterrupted line of fire if necessary. "Only, was it me, I'd think *real* careful afore I made what could be a bad mistake. One thing I learned when I wore a badge under Cap'n Fog in Quiet Town,* he's liable to get tolerable riled, happen he's told that somebody's *lynched* one of his men without being guilty."

"You wore a badge for Cap'n Fog?" asked one of the crowd.

"In Quiet Town," Doc confirmed.

"Then you're—!" the questioner began.

"Doc Leroy," the cowhand finished for the man. "And us

* Told in Quiet Town.—J.T.E.

boys of the Wedge aren't any too taken with *friends* getting lynched, either, comes to that."

Once again the spokesman realized that his associates were impressed by what they were hearing. The Wedge was known to be a tough and salty outfit in its own right, with Doc Leroy's name ranking high on the roll of its employees. Unlike Silkie Roelich, a number of the crowd had heard of his ability with a gun. In fact, the story of what had happened at the Man on the Wall Saloon had reached them and lost nothing in the telling. So they appreciated the position. By his actions and words the pallid-faced cowhand had aligned himself with the deputy sheriff. Even without the rest of the Wedge on hand, his was a backing that could not be taken lightly.

Nor had the crowd overlooked the emphasis Doc had placed when saying "lynched." It was a word that had *very* ugly connotations. No matter how much they might try to justify their intentions as avenging the murder of a well-liked and respected member of the community, every one of them knew—even if he would not have admitted it openly—that they were usurping rather than furthering the interests of justice.

"Thanking you kindly for your interest, gents," Tragg said, reading the crowd's emotions and satisfied that there was no immediate danger. "Only, there's nothing more to be done tonight. Happen I take out a posse in the morning. I'll call on you-all. Let's get going, Doc, Tarbrush."

Giving the men on the sidewalk no chance to air further views, the deputy started his horse moving. Accompanied by the buckboard and the cowhand he made his way along the street without a backward glance. However, as they reached their destination, he looked and discovered that the crowd had not yet reentered the Ranchero Saloon.

"One thing I don't get," the spokesman growled, seeing a chance of earning the money he had been promised by keeping the crowd stirred up. "Why's Tragg taking the nigger into the jailhouse if he didn't kill good ole Doctor Gol-licker?"

"Yeah!" agreed the second speaker, being equally desir-ous to acquire the pay they had been offered. "There's an-other thing. When the OD Connected's crew went through to fetch the cattle, I don't recall no nigger riding with 'em."

"Hey!" yelped a third man, oozing indignation. "There wasn't one. That sneaky son of a bitch Tragg's lied to us."

"He'd only do that to save the nigger's skin!" the spokes-man declared. "Come on, let's go down there and find out what's doing."

"Hell, yes!" supported the second agitator, when there was a distinct hesitancy displayed toward accepting the sug-gestions. "We're all law-abiding folks 'n' have a right to know whether the peace officers're doing right by us. Come on. Let's go and make sure."

Given such a spurious justification and excuse the rest of the crowd set off on the pair's heels.

"There's trouble!" Marshal Arthur Gormley announced, coming from his office as Doc Leroy followed Jervis Tragg and Tarbrush into the jailhouse. "Don't ask me how, but the word's got out about Doctor Gollicker being killed and feel-ings're running high."

"Saw some of it on the way in," the deputy sheriff replied.

"So that's why you've brought the nigger in?" Gormley said, more as a statement than a question.

"I don't follow you," Tragg drawled.

"You've arrested him, haven't you?" Gormley elaborated.

"Nope," Tragg answered.

"Why not?" the marshal demanded.

"Mostly because I've nothing to arrest him for," Tragg explained.

"Damn it!" Gormley growled. "Doctor Gollicker's been murdered—"

"Which doesn't prove Tarbrush here did it," Tragg pointed out.

"It's all over town that he did!" Gormley stated. "And, happen you don't throw him in the pokey, there'll be some's'll figure on handing him his needings."

"And you'd let it happen?" Tragg inquired.

"What can I do if he's let go roaming the streets?" Gormley countered, remembering the instructions he had received from Silkie Roelich and paving the way to carrying them out.

"There's some might say keep the peace," Doc Leroy commented dryly. Glancing out of the window, his voice lost its bantering tone. "Looks like those yahoos aren't satisfied, Jervis. They're coming."

"There!" Gormley almost yelped. "It's starting already!"

"And it's going to be stopped," Tragg stated, then looked at the young Negro. "I've no call to think you've done anything wrong, friend. But it's better for now that I have the marshal put you in a cell until morning."

"That's all right with me," Tarbrush declared, having gained complete faith in the deputy's integrity and judgment. "Fact being, I was wondering where I'd get me a bed for the night."

"Will you show him into a cell, Marshal?" Tragg requested, wanting to keep the crowd under observation. Then his voice took on a harder note as he continued, "Just bear in mind that he's *not* under arrest, only in what's known as protective custody. He rides for the OD Connected and I don't reckon's how General Hardin or Cap'n Fog'd take it kind was anything to happen to him."

"General Hardin—?" Gormley repeated worriedly.

"Or Cap'n Fog," Tragg drawled, deciding that the marshal was as impressed by his falsehood as the crowd had been.

The deputy's supposition was correct. Accepting that he had been told the truth with respect to Tarbrush's employer, Gormley was deeply perturbed. However, as he was escorting the Negro to the door that gave access to the row of cells at the rear of the building, he drew one slight consolation. No matter what happened, he would be able to claim in exculpation that he had acted upon Tragg's instructions and the blame would be diverted from him.

"Go down to that end cell," Gormley ordered.

"Sure thing," Tarbrush assented.

Such was the young Negro's trust in Jervis Tragg that he gave no thought to the fact that the cell he entered differed in one major aspect from the rest. While the barred windows were set high in the others, this one's was at the same level as those in the offices. Without as much as a backward glance when the marshal closed the door, he sat down. Instead of fastening the lock Gormley turned and walked back to rejoin the deputy and the cowhand.

Standing in the darkness Toby Hooper watched Tarbrush being incarcerated and let out a low grunt of satisfaction. Everything was going as Silkie Roelich had promised it would. Now all that remained was for him to carry out the task to which he had been assigned by the boss gun.

Sliding out his right-hand Army Colt and easing back its hammer to fully cocked, Hooper advanced with care so as to avoid making any unnecessary sound. He waited until the marshal had left for the front of the building, closing the dividing door in passing, then moved around until he could see into the cell. There would, he decided, be nothing difficult in what he had come to do. So he started to raise the weapon, ready to align its barrel at the Negro who was sitting on the bunk.

"Drop it!" snapped a voice.

Spitting out a curse, Hooper turned. Even as his brain was registering that the speaker did not sound masculine, he saw a shape in the shadows of the jail's outhouse. His Colt bellowed and he heard the sound of its bullet striking wood instead of human flesh. Thumbing back the hammer, he tried to correct his aim.

Flame lanced from the darkness and a lighter crack than the deep cough of the Army Colt rang out. Flying with greater accuracy than Hooper had attained, the bullet from alongside the backhouse ripped into his head. Spun around by the impact, he released his weapon and it discharged as it fell. He knew nothing of that, for he was dead by the time he had followed it to the ground.

Having saved Tarbrush's life, the figure by the outhouse did not wait for praise or thanks. Instead, swinging around and emerging into the moonlight, it proved to be the slender young woman who had twice come to Roelich's notice. Thrusting what looked like a Navy Colt into her vanity bag (she was no longer carrying the parasol) she hurried toward two unlit buildings. Looking back to make sure that she was not observed, she reached the darkness of the alley separating them.

And walked straight into the arms of a gigantic figure that was standing there!

CHAPTER NINE

YOU COULD'VE GOTTEN KILLED

"Some blasted guide you-all are turning out to be," stated Captain Dustine Edward Marsden Fog, C.S.A., bringing the seventeen-hand paint stallion he was riding, and the lightly loaded pack horse he was leading, to a halt. Tilting back his black Texas-style Stetson to show some of his curly, dusty blond-colored hair, he continued to study his companion in a sardonic fashion as he elaborated, "From what I remember, you claimed that we didn't need to follow any winding trail and could come straight overland, seeing's how you know every inch of the Rio Grande country like the back of your hand."

"What do you-all reckon Belle wants from us, Dusty?" the Ysabel Kid inquired, deliberately ignoring the comment, as he stopped his equally large, magnificent, and masculine white mount.

"We'll likely find out when—or *if*—we ever make it to Bannock's Ford," the first speaker replied. "And don't try to change the subject."

Taken on purely external appearances little suggested why Dusty Fog's name should have produced such an effect when it was mentioned to the would-be lynch mob in the town. There was hardly anything by which a casual observer might have deduced how he had attained his already legendary fame. By all the accepted criteria a man who had achieved so much in a comparatively few years should have been a veritable giant of near godlike proportions and description.*

From his Stetson-covered head to his high-heeled and sharp-toed tan-colored boots,† Dusty Fog measured barely five feet six inches. While his functional cowhand-style clothing was expensive and well made, he somehow contrived to give the impression that the garments were somebody better-favored's castoffs. Nor did the two bone-handled Colt 1860 Army revolvers riding butts forward on his brown gun belt make him any more noticeable as he lounged with easy grace on his top-quality range saddle and addressed the taller man at his side.

Despite his generally insignificant appearance a more careful examination would have revealed clues to suggest the small Texan's true potential. His tanned face was good looking without being eye catching, but a closer scrutiny would have found a strength of will and intelligence in its lines. They were not the features of a weakling whose ego had been boosted by family influence. While he was of small stature, there was a breadth to his shoulders and a slimming at the waist that denoted a muscular development beyond the average. Made by a master leather craftsman the carefully designed holsters of his gun belt explained how he could produce the Colts—aided by being completely ambidextrous, a trait he had perfected in part to take attention from his lack of height—with almost sight-defying rapidity. There was yet a further pointer to be gained from his mount. Large, spirited, and powerful without being cumbersome, only a rider of outstanding ability could cope with it. In fact, it was the self-same animal that—before Dusty had

* For the benefit of new readers details of Captain Dustine Edward Marsden "Dusty" Fog's background and special abilities are given in APPENDIX ONE. —J.T.E.

† The sharp toes of a cowhand's boots allow them to be inserted or removed swiftly and easily from the stirrup irons and the high heels give security by spiking into the ground when the wearer is roping on foot. —J.T.E.

tamed and trained it—had crippled General Ole Devil Hardin, a first-rate horseman in his own right.*

All in all there was much more to Dusty Fog than met the eye!

More than one man who had dismissed the small Texan as an unimportant and insignificant nobody had come to regret making such an erroneous judgment.

In addition to having heard of Dusty's reputation, a factor that had exerted considerable pressure in the potential lynch mob's desire to avoid antagonizing him had been the knowledge that he could call upon the services of an exceptionally tough, loyal, and fight-wise ranch crew. That applied particularly to the members of the OD Connected's floating outfit† in general and most of all where the man to whom he was talking was concerned.

Yet, taken on first impressions, once again there was little upon the surface to show why this should be.

Touching six feet in height, the Ysabel Kid had a lean frame that possessed a whipcord strength. His hair was the shining black of a crow's wing, and apart from his red hazel eyes supplying a suggestion of his real nature, there was an expression of almost babyish innocence on his handsome, Indian-dark features. From his hat down to his boots, including the gun belt and leather vest, everything he wore was black. On his right thigh, its worn walnut grips turned to the front for a low cavalry-twist draw, hung an old Colt 1848 First Model Dragoon revolver. However, the .44 caliber, four-pound, one-ounce handgun was not his only—or even main—weapon. Sheathed at the left side of his belt was a massive ivory-handled James Black bowie knife, with the aid of which he had gained his Comanche man-name, Cuchilo. In moments of danger he tended to rely upon the cold steel at close quarters. Over a long range he was just as effective with the Winchester Model 1866 rifle, which at that moment

* Told in the "The Paint" episode of THE FASTEST GUN IN TEXAS.—J.T.E.

† New readers: for an explanation of a floating outfit's function, see APPENDIX TWO, Footnote 4.—J.T.E.

was being carried in its boot on the left side of his white stallion's saddle.

Like his employer the Kid was not a person to be taken lightly. In fact, his birth and upbringing among the Pehnane Comanche Indians* made him a very good friend—or an implacable and deadly enemy.

"Well?" Dusty prompted, when some thirty seconds had ticked by without bringing him an answer.

"There's some's'd say changing the subject's better'n lying," the Indian-dark young man declared, sounding virtuous. "Which I'm among 'em. Specially when I can't think up a good one."

"Don't let *that* bother you," Dusty ordered. "I mean about thinking up a *good* lie. You *never* have yet."

"That's my Nemenuh† blood's does it," the Kid said, adopting an air redolent of patience and resignation. Then, having devoted a little more time to contemplation, he went on, "All I can figure's how you-all must've heard me wrong. What I said was's how I knowed every inch of the parts of the Rio Grande's I'd crossed at. Which Bannock Ford ain't one of 'em. Pappy and me never had no call to go through there."

"That figures," Dusty answered dryly. "You might have, only you was running contraband *both* ways and sneaking out of paying the due and lawful duties to the customs officers in either country."

"Them duties might've been lawful," the Kid countered. "Trouble being that every son-of-a-bitch place pappy 'n' me came through, no matter how hard we looked, they just wasn't due on account of nobody being around to pay 'em to."

"Lordy lord!" The small Texan sighed, looking upward as

* Details of the Ysabel Kid's background and special abilities are given in APPENDIX THREE.—J.T.E.
† Nemenuh: "The People," the Comanche Indians' name for their nation. —J.T.E.

if in search of divine guidance. "I'm beginning to wish that I'd just accepted what he told me at first."

"Most folks get round to feeling that way," the Kid declared unashamedly.

"Most folks aren't lucky enough to be able to have *you-all* riding the blister end of a shovel when they get you back to home," Dusty warned and, taking no notice of the other's sotto voce comment of "Sore loser," gazed around before going on, "That stream down there among the trees can't be the Rio Grande."

"Likely ends up in it, though," the Kid guessed. "Was I asked, that is."

"You *wasn't,*" Dusty stated. "I've an idea."

"Which mean's how *I'm* going to be made to do some work," the Kid suggested.

"While I'm watering the horses at that stream," Dusty continued, as if the interruption had never been uttered, *"somebody's* going to head up that hill there and find out if he can see anything of Bannock's from the top."

"Like I said," the Kid sighed, *"I'm* going to be made to do some work. Let's get moving ole Shadow, afore he tells me to do it afoot."

Riding in the opposite direction to his companion, Dusty found his thoughts were turning to the matter on which the other had tried to change the subject. The telegraph message that had brought them from the OD Connected was brief and had given no hint as to the reason it had been dispatched. However, Ole Devil and he knew the sender well enough to have accepted that the cause must be of considerable importance. So the Kid and he had set off to find out what it might be. If they should require further assistance, two more members of the floating outfit would soon be passing through Bannock's Ford as part of a trail crew collecting a herd of cattle purchased from a ranchero in Mexico.

Passing through the woodland, which was fairly open at that point in spite of becoming denser farther downstream, Dusty dismounted on the bank of the small river. As the telegraph message had asked that he reach Bannock's Ford before the end of the month and there were still seven days left, he and the Kid had not been hurrying. So he knew that he could allow the horses to drink straightaway without it being detrimental to their health. Removing their bits he stepped aside to let them commence and watched his companion carrying out his instructions.

By the time that the animals had drunk their fill, the small Texan saw the Kid was riding down the slope. While wondering if the mission had been successful, the sound of leaves rustling and branches being broken diverted his attention. Ready to draw either a revolver or the Winchester Model 1866 carbine from the paint's saddle boot, he discovered that the noise was produced by a human being pushing through a clump of bushes instead of going around.

Advancing with staggering steps the man entered a patch of open ground. Before Dusty could make out more than that he was an exceptionally large, muscular, and completely bald Negro, he stumbled. Clasping his hands to his head he collapsed to crouch with his face pressed against the bulky trunk of a silver maple tree. Although his massive frame began to shudder violently, no sound came from him.

Showing no hesitation the small Texan began to walk forward. However, despite the Negro's noisy approach through the undergrowth and his apparent debility, he did not rule out the possibility of a trap. He still did not arm himself, but he scanned the bushes and trees beyond the crouching figure. There was neither sound nor movement to suggest that the Negro had companions close by. Nor did he give the slightest sign of knowing that somebody was coming toward him.

Satisfied that the Negro was alone, Dusty studied him carefully in the hope of discovering some clue to explain his behavior. Not until he was fairly close did he notice the metal bands around the man's wrists. Then he was struck by an observation that brought him to a halt while a few feet still separated them. Although the shackles had been in position for some considerable time, the ragged edges of the left side link glinted in a way that warned the chain had been snapped from it recently.

"Hey, feller," Dusty began, realizing that—although he had not heard there was such a thing in the vicinity—the broken shackles might mean the man had escaped from a prison's chain gang. "What's wr—?"

At the small Texan's first word the Negro removed his hands from his head and it swung around. As soon as his staring eyes reached the white face, his mouth opened in a soundless snarl that showed off his awesome teeth. Lurching erect with great rapidity, he flung himself forward and his huge hands reached out like the talons of some enormous, hideous bird of prey.

Such was the shock Dusty received from his first clear view of the gigantic black man's ravaged features that he could not prevent himself from taking an involuntary and hurried step to the rear. Despite that, his instinct for self-preservation and superbly attuned reflexes caused him to respond to the threat with barely any need for conscious thought. Taking his weight on his forward foot he whipped up the other in a power-packed kick. The toe of the swiftly rising boot took his assailant between the legs with considerable force.

But produced no observable effect!

Without making a sound, or showing the slightest sign of pain, the Negro continued his attack. Amazed by the lack of response to what should have been at least an exceptionally painful impact against the most vulnerable portion of the male anatomy, Dusty's normally lightning-fast reactions were momentarily numbed. Before he could make another move, or even return his foot to the ground, the Negro's enormous left hand closed on his throat in a grip such as he had never encountered. Caught off balance and on one leg, he was knocked over.

Going down, Dusty felt his hat slipping. It was prevented from falling all the way off by its *barbiquejo*. However, although it acted as a cushion between his head and the ground, he landed supine with a force that drove all the breath and cohesive thought from him. Following him down the Negro straddled his torso. He was still gripped by the hand—which had the cold, clammy feel of a dead fish and the strength of a bear trap's jaws—around the throat and watched the other clenched fist rising for a blow that would be powered by the tremendous muscles of the black arm and shoulder. Yet, in his present physical condition, he could do nothing to defend himself.

The blow was not delivered!

While still some distance away the Kid had seen the Negro and duplicated Dusty's thoughts on the possibility of a trap. So, should one be contemplated by the huge man, he had made preparations to help deal with it. Unlike the majority of Texans, as his work mainly comprised riding scout, he used one-piece reins. Allowing them to fall onto the saddle horn, he slipped free and fed a bullet into the chamber of his Winchester while searching the woodland for any suggestion that the Negro had confederates lurking close by. Then he watched the attack being launched upon his companion, but at first felt little concern.

During the years they had ridden together, the Kid had witnessed many examples of how effectively the small Texan could protect himself against larger, heavier, and stronger men. Nor had he always needed to rely upon his weapons, swiftly as he could draw and fire the Colts, to cope with them. In fact, the training in certain barehanded fighting techniques he had received from Ole Devil Hardin's Japanese valet gave him a considerable advantage as they were so little known in the western world.*

Having such knowledge it came as a surprise to the Kid when he saw how the Negro accepted the kick and brought Dusty down with so little difficulty. What was more, he could

* New readers can find the explanation of how this came about in the last footnote of APPENDIX ONE.—J.T.E.

see that the small Texan was temporarily incapacitated by the fall and unable to deal with the situation.

Flowing swiftly upward the butt of the Winchester nestled against the Kid's right shoulder. Without offering to stop the white stallion's swift walk, he was already taking sight along the barrel when the brass plate touched his shirt. Almost as soon as the weapon steadied, his forefinger tightened on the trigger. In spite of the rapidity with which he had moved, he knew there was only one way in which he could save his companion from a serious injury and aimed accordingly.

Even as Dusty was trying to take some action on his own behalf, he saw the Negro's head jerk violently and almost simultaneously with the sound of the Kid's rifle reaching his ears. The side of the bald black skull burst open as the flat-nosed .44 caliber bullet passed through. Instantly, the raised fist collapsed instead of being propelled downward. The choking grasp left the small Texan's throat and his lifeless assailant toppled from him. Shaking his head and gasping in air he managed to roll in the opposite direction. By the time the Kid arrived, he was sufficiently recovered to sit up and rub his neck gently.

"Are you all right, amigo?" the Kid inquired solicitously, springing from his stallion's back as it came to a stop.

"I am now, *gracias*," Dusty replied, making a wry face. "That was one tolerable tough jasper, I'll tell you."

"I've only seen one's can lick him for heft 'n' muscle," the Kid declared. "And even Mark wouldn't've took a kick like you gave him without showing it'd been felt. Which some's say you was a mite careless walking up to him the way you did. You could've gotten killed."

"Now he tells me!" Dusty groaned and, accepting his companion's offered left hand, came to his feet. Glancing at the body he went on, "Lordy lord, Lon, I've never seen anything like his face."

"He for sure isn't the best-looking son of a bitch I've ever come across," the Kid declared, having turned his gaze to the Negro's features. "Which brings up something else,

Dusty. He's got shackles on his wrists, so where'd you-all reckon he come from?"

"I couldn't start to guess," the small Texan replied, still fingering his throat gingerly. "So we'll tote him into Bannock's on the pack horse and leave it to the local law to find out."

The sound of gunfire from the rear of the jailhouse took Deputy Sheriff Jervis Tragg's, Doc Leroy's, and Marshal Arthur Gormley's attention from the crowd at the front of it. They exchanged glances. Even Gormley was startled, but for a different reason from the other two. He had expected only a single shot and was wondering why there had been more, clearly from different types of weapons.

"Come on!" Tragg snapped, drawing his Colt—a move duplicated by the cowhand—before the municipal peace officer could reach any conclusion over the unexpected development.

Followed by Doc and Gormley, who did not take the precaution of arming himself, the deputy ran to the door in the dividing wall. Ignoring the shouts of the men outside he jerked it open and went through. Glancing around he found that Tarbrush was standing alongside the window of the cell and holding a Navy Colt.

So, gazing over Doc's and Tragg's shoulders, did Gormley.

"Watch out!" the marshal screeched, wishing that he had drawn his own weapon as he realized what an opportunity was being offered. "The nigger's got a gun!"

Although Tarbrush had armed himself instinctively when he had heard the shooting, Gormley's words warned him that his action might be misinterpreted. So he tossed the revolver on to the bunk and hurriedly raised his hands level with his shoulders.

"What happened?" Tragg demanded, striding toward the cell.

"I dunno," the young Negro replied. "But it wasn't me's did the shooting."

As he shoved at the door, the only thing to surprise the deputy at finding it was unlocked was that his municipal colleague had had sufficient tact, particularly when a colored man was involved, to leave it unsecured. Entering the cell he took up the Colt and sniffed at its muzzle to find, as he expected, that it had not been fired. One of the shots had come from a weapon of similar caliber, but was discharged at some distance outside the building. Furthermore, if Tarbrush had used his handgun, the smoke from the detonated powder would not yet have dispersed and there was no trace of it in the air.

"Come with us!" Tragg ordered, turning on his heel.

Leaving the deputy to investigate the Negro, but keeping an eye on Gormley—about whom he harbored certain suspicions—Doc Leroy had gone to the rear door. Finding it was bolted, he threw them free and drew it open. However, remembering the training he had been given by Dusty Fog while serving as a deputy town marshal in Quiet Town, he did not go out immediately. Instead, he paused clear of the opening until Tragg and Tarbrush were coming toward him. Then he lunged through, his Colt swinging toward the end of the building in which the Negro's cell was situated. His gaze went to the body that was sprawled on the ground and turned from it to survey his surroundings.

"Hey!" Tarbrush shouted, as he and Tragg joined the cowhand and he looked at the dead man. "That's one of them fellers I met on the trail!"

"Uh-huh!" the deputy grunted. "Toby Hooper from the Island Mission. But who dropped him?"

"Whoever it was hasn't stayed around to be thanked," Doc answered, making an accurate guess at what had happened. "I didn't see or hear—"

"Over there!" Tragg snapped, pointing his Colt toward the two deserted buildings beyond the outhouse.

"Take it easy!" Doc advised, looking at the tall man who came from the dark alley between the buildings. "I know him."

"So do I," Tragg admitted, lowering his weapon. "Hey, Mark, what're you doing here?"

"Looking for Doc there," the big newcomer answered, his voice a deep and well educated southern drawl. "I heard shooting down this way."

"There was some," the deputy conceded. "Did you see anybody?"

"Heard somebody running off," the tall man replied. "Couldn't say where for sure, but no man's come by me."

CHAPTER TEN

HE'S BEEN DEAD FOR AT LEAST A MONTH

There was a puzzled frown on the face of Deputy Sheriff Jervis Tragg as he entered the Jolene Hotel's dining room on the morning after Tarbrush's arrival in Bannock's Ford. Three of the men with whom the peace officer had an appointment were sitting at a table eating breakfast.

Although there had been no clue as to the identity of Toby Hooper's killer, Tragg had no doubts about what he was up to when he was shot. However, why he had tried to murder the young Negro was still a mystery. Nor, as they had left town before he could reach them, had the deputy been able to question Silkie Roelich and Ivan Petrov. One thing had seemed certain to him. Hooper was motivated by a stronger reason than merely a desire to avenge the death of Doctor Gollicker.

Learning the identity of the man who had arrived shortly after Hooper's death was a major factor in causing the crowd to decide against trying to lynch Tarbrush. Not only was he known to be a leading member of Ole Devil Hardin's floating outfit, but Mark Counter had a reputation of being second only to Dusty Fog in matters *pistolero,* and when it came to fighting with bare hands, his fame was even higher. So his presence had proved a stout inducement to keeping the peace. Furthermore, the arrival of the small Texan and the Ysabel Kid with their grisly burden had been proof that the young Negro was telling the truth about the Doctor's killer.

Despite the delivery of the body having established Tarbrush's innocence, it had added to rather than solving the mystery. When Tragg learned that the two men whom he suspected might be able to supply information were not available, he accepted Dusty Fog's suggestion that any further investigation be postponed until there was daylight in which to conduct it. So, arranging a rendezvous for the following morning, he and the cowhands had gone their separate ways. Tarbrush had requested that he be allowed to spend the night in the jailhouse and the deputy had given his agreement.

"Good morning, Jervis," the small Texan greeted. "I'm sorry we started without you, but these two aren't worth a cuss until they've been fed, and not often even then."

"Morning," Tragg answered, drawing out a chair and sitting down. "I've just been fixing for some food to be sent over to Tarbrush."

"Now, me," the Kid drawled, "I thought that all peace officers stayed in bed till noon most days."

While the third cowhand at the table did not speak, he gave an amiable nod. For all that, the deputy thought he looked a trifle uneasy and wondered, if such was the case, why he was.

In many respects Mark Counter had the kind of physical appearance popular conception imagined Dusty Fog should possess. Six feet three inches tall, with tremendously broad shoulders, a lean waist, and Herculean muscular development, his hair was wavy golden blond and his face almost classically handsome. He wore his expensive range clothes with a greater élan than the small Texan and, in fact, was an accepted arbiter of cowhand fashion in much the same way that his taste in uniforms had been extensively copied by the other young officers in the Confederate cavalry during the War of Secession.

However, as Tragg was well aware, there was much more than a wealthy and very strong young dandy about the blond giant.* So he was curious about Mark's attitude, for which he felt that he was in some way responsible.

"Here's another who sleeps late in the morning," the Kid went on, before the deputy could think of a way to satisfy his curiosity regarding the blond giant. "Let's see what *his* excuse is."

"Dusty," Doc Leroy said, crossing to the table and looking, if possible, even more pallid and studious than usual, "you know that feller Lon had to shoot last night?"

"I'm not likely to forget *him* any too soon," the small Texan replied.

"I thought there was something strange about him when you brought him in and told us what happened," Doc continued. "So I've been down to the undertaker's and took a closer look. You'll *never* guess what I found out."

"Which being the case, there's not a whole heap of point in us trying," the Kid put in, realizing that only something exceptionally out of the ordinary could have produced such a show of emotion from the slender cowhand. "So why not just tell us?"

"That's what I'm aiming to, given the chance," Doc answered. "You shot him in the head not too late last night—"

"It'll be late *tonight* afore he gets round to telling us what's up," the Kid groaned.

"What I was fixing to say," Doc announced, eyeing the interrupter with an air of pained martyrdom, "is that you-all shot him through the head *last night*—but he's been dead for at least a month."

If the Wedge cowhand had hoped that his words would create a very noticeable sensation, he would have been disappointed. Not that he had expected to, knowing the caliber of the men with whom he was dealing. However, he felt that he had evoked what was—for them—strong reactions. Dusty's knife stopped cutting through a piece of ham for a moment. Although Mark had a cup at his lips, he refrained

* Details of Mark Counter's background and special qualifications are given in APPENDIX TWO.—J.T.E.

from drinking for just as long. Opening, the Kid's mouth closed again without any sound coming out and Tragg paused briefly before picking up the coffeepot.

"You'd best drive that one through again, Doc," Dusty requested. "It went by too fast to get a rope on it."

"Like I said," Doc obliged, sitting down and hanging his hat on the back of the chair. "He's been dead for maybe a month."

"How the hell could he have been dead that long when he was walking around last night, damn it?" Tragg demanded, although his every instinct suggested that the cowhand was not joking.

"Don't ask *me,* I'm only telling you what I found out," Doc replied irritably. Then he gave a slight shrug and darted an apologetic glance at the deputy, "I hope it's all right with you-all, Jervis, but I told the undertaker that *you'd* asked me to carry out an autopsy."

"It's way too late now, even if it wasn't," Tragg pointed out, but he showed no animosity. In fact, while realizing that the findings were adding to the puzzle, he was pleased it had been done. "And I don't reckon that he'll have any kinfolks coming around to complain."

"Happen he has and they look like him," the Kid drawled, "I'd sure's hell listen when they get to doing it."

"You'll sure's hell be listening to *you* digging a new outhouse hole when we get back to home, happen you don't keep shut!" Dusty warned, then returned his attention to Doc. "Can you-all make it a li'l mite plainer for us poor li'l ole half-smart Texas boys, amigo?"

"I opened him up like Pappy taught me," the slender cowhand said, yet the twist of distaste to his lips belied the unemotional way in which he was speaking. "The first thing I noticed was that he smelled a whole lot worse than he should've done—"

"I said *that* last night," the Kid injected, then raised his hands in a gesture of surrender, although he had commented on the subject while Dusty and he were loading the corpse onto the pack horse. "All right, all right. I *know*. Get shut, Lon!"

"Ignore him and he'll maybe go away," Mark suggested. "Not that it'll help. We've been trying for years, but he's still hanging around—or should be."

"I notice the blasted white folks don't get told to keep shut," the Kid commented sotto voce. "Hot damn! Us Injuns oughtn't never to've let the Pilgrim Fathers land."

"And I always thought the Wedge was bad." Doc sighed, thankful for the brief respite. He was not relishing the recollection of the unpleasant task he had carried out and, guessing how he was feeling, his amigos had created the diversion for him. Then he became serious and went on, "That was only the start of it. His heart looked sort of shriveled, but it's been pumping I'm damned if I know what kind of blood around. I've never seen its like before. It was the same with his lungs. They weren't right, but they'd been working, too, I'd say. Nothing else had for a fair spell, though. The stomach—"

"I don't reckon I'll bother with any breakfast," Tragg declared, when the sight of a waiter approaching to take orders brought the slim cowhand's explanation to a temporary halt.

"Or me," Doc seconded.

Turning in a disinterested fashion the waiter ambled away, but the cowhand did not have the opportunity to continue. Coming into the dining room the young woman who was known as Elvira Porterham glanced around and crossed to where he was sitting with his companions. She was dressed in much the same fashion as she had been the previous night, with the parasol and vanity bag in her hands. There was more than a hint of a strong-willed personality to her beautiful features despite the hesitant way in which she was looking at the men.

"Excuse me for imposing, gentlemen," the woman said in a pleasant upper-class Deep South accent and, looking at

Mark as he and his companions came to their feet, continued, "I believe you are Captain Fog?"

"There's no need for *that*, Belle," Dusty drawled, and nodded in the deputy's direction. "We can trust Jervis."

"So I was told when I was given the assignment," the woman admitted, losing the suggestion of hesitancy and turned her gaze to the peace officer. "But I always like to get a second—and closer—opinion. Would you introduce us, please, Dusty?"

"Belle, this is Deputy Sheriff Jervis Tragg," the small Texan drawled. "Jervis, meet Belle Boyd."

"B-Belle Boyd?" the deputy repeated, staring at the young woman who was just as much a legend as Dusty in her own life time.* *"You're* the Rebel Spy?"

"Disappointing, isn't it." The young woman smiled, offering Tragg her hand. "I work for the United States Secret Service now, though. I'm sorry that I haven't made myself known to you before now, Jervis, but I didn't see you in town until last night."

"I only got here yesterday afternoon," the peace officer replied, feeling the firmness and latent power in Belle's grip.

"Sit down, please, gentlemen," the woman requested. "May I join you?"

"This'll be as good a place as any for us to talk," Dusty stated and, waiting until Mark had drawn out a chair for their new guest and they were all seated, went on, "You were right about what Hooper was up to behind the jailhouse, Jervis. And you don't need to look any farther for his killer."

"That's not a pleasant way to put it, Dusty," Belle protested. "In fact, I'd rather have tried to take him alive if I could have done it without letting it be known that I was involved. You arrived just too late, Mark."

"Heh-heh!" the Kid sniggered, eyeing the blond giant delightedly. "It's mostly *me's* gets the blame."

* Details of Belle Boyd's background, special qualifications, and how she gained the sobriquet "the Rebel Spy" are given in Appendix Five.—J.T.E.

"That doesn't surprise *me,"* Belle countered. "From all I remember, you mostly deserve to get it."

"I reckon I'd best get told the whole story," Tragg said coldly, drawing conclusions for which he did not particularly care out of his remembrance of the previous night's incidents.

"When Belle met up with me in the alley back of the jailhouse, just after she'd stopped Hooper gunning Tarbrush down, she asked me not to mention seeing her to that butt-dragging town clown," Mark commenced. "And he was never far enough away from us for me to be able to say anything to you-all afore we split up."

"I told Mark it could wait until this morning," Dusty announced, being the kind of a man who was willing to admit any responsibility that he had assumed.

"It isn't *you* that I mistrust, Jervis," Belle declared, as the deputy's gaze swung to her. "But I've seen enough of Gormley to want to avoid letting him even suspect I'm not what I'm supposed to be."

"Comes to a point," Doc went on, grinning at the peace officer, "you-all didn't exactly put *all* your cards face up when you was dealing with him."

"For shame," chided the Kid. "If there's one thing I can't stand, it's lawmen's don't play square with each other—or any other kind, afore somebody else says it."

"Damned if they're not ganging up on poor li'l ole *me* now!" Tragg exclaimed, his good humor returning. His tone was more cordial as he requested, "All right, so what's going on around here?"

"Is it all right if we order breakfast first?" Belle asked. "It will look more natural for us to be eating while we're talking."

"Go to it," Tragg offered, the pangs of hunger having returned now that Doc's description of the dead Negro had been temporarily forgotten.

"I'll give you all I can," Belle promised, after food and more coffee had been served. "I owe you that much, Jervis, but there's a lot that I don't know. What it boils down to is that the government of Haiti is raising hell with Congress about Professor Morbeus. It seems that he stole something they set great store by while he was over there."

"Morbeus, huh?" Tragg grunted. "Hooper and the other pair I went looking for last night work for him out to the Island Mission, Dusty."

"Do, huh?" the small Texan said, almost absently.

"I surely hate to sound ignorant—" the Kid began.

"Why not?" Mark challenged, sharing his Indian-dark amigo's knowledge that Dusty was thinking of something. "You mostly do."

"But where-at's thishere 'Haiti' place?" the Kid finished, showing no sign of acknowledging the blond giant's comment.

"It's a small country," Belle supplied. "Covers about half of the island that used to be called Hispaniola, out between the Atlantic Ocean and the Caribbean Sea."

"Wherever *they* might be," the Kid sniffed, although he had a pretty good idea. During the last years of the War of Secession he and his father had delivered cargoes from Confederate blockade runners who sailed out of ports in the West Indies. "Shucks, happen it's only an itty-bitty country, I don't see why Congress'd raise too much fuss and sweat over what their government might think."

"The population is descended from mulattoes and Negro slaves," Belle elaborated. "They drove out the French and set up their own country in the early eighteen hundreds.*

"So *that's* why Congress is ready to oblige," the Kid drawled sardonically, before the young woman could continue with her explanation. "Only, I don't see why General Han—your boss, figured it needed *you-all* down here to tend to things. Seeing's it knowed this professor hombre's got whatever them Haiti folks want back, the local law could easy enough go along and fetch him in with it."

* After years of unrest and open rebellion against France, independence was declared and the name "Haiti" adopted on January 1, 1804.—J.T.E.

"It isn't that easy," Belle corrected, pleased by the tribute to her abilities and with the way in which the Kid had avoided mentioning the head of the United States Secret Service, General Philo Handiman, by name.

"Why not?" the Indian-dark Texan demanded. "Hell"—he directed a mischievous grin at the young woman—"which's language I wouldn't use was there a *lady* present—I've heard tell's how some of them soft-shells and liberradicals up to Washington don't take kind to peace officers treating thieves and murderers mean. But, seeing's how it's *colored folk's* he's robbed, they'd likely say it serves him right no matter how Jervis goes after him."

"There's more to it than just that," Tragg stated, despite agreeing with the Kid's comments about the kind of double standards employed by "soft-shells" and "liberradicals"— liberal-intellectuals with radical tendencies—where such matters were concerned. "For one thing the Island Mission isn't in Kinney County and the sheriff's office has no jurisdiction there. Fact being, there's some who reckon it's not even part of these here United States."

"That's true enough, Lon," Belle confirmed. "Don't tell me that you've never heard of the Island Mission?"

"Pappy and me never had any call to go there," the Kid admitted. "But I hear tell it's about five–six miles upriver from here, built on an island where the Rio Grande spreads out to make like a lake. And that the fathers who ran it pulled out during the fussing with ole 'Cheno' Cortina back in sixty 'n' they never came back."

"It's exactly in the *center* of the river," Belle elaborated. "So the Mexican government has just as much right as we have to say it belongs to them. But, particularly after the mission closed, neither country felt it was worth the trouble of trying to claim sovereign rights over it."

"How did this Professor Morbeus get hold of it, Belle?" Mark inquired.

"He bought it from the religious order who owned and

built it," the young woman replied. "You've been out there, Jervis?"

"Why, sure," the deputy replied, drawing satisfaction from the words having been more of a statement than a question. He had completely lost his earlier annoyance and was impressed by Belle's obvious competence, realizing that she had earned her nickname "the Rebel Spy" on merit and ability. "The sheriff and I went just after he'd moved in, but we didn't get out to the island. The professor met us on the bank and showed us a couple of letters saying's how the mission was his private property and all peace officers were to respect his privacy. Going by the folks's'd signed them, he's got some right influential amigos in both Washington and Mexico City."

"He has," Belle agreed. "That's what makes dealing with him so difficult."

"Thinking on what the Kid said about soft-shells," Tragg drawled, "will those jaspers who signed his letter of introduction stand by him under these circumstances?"

"They are doing so," Belle declared.

"Have you got any idea why?" Tragg asked. "Like the Kid said, they're not usually willing to stand by a white man when he's up against colored folk."

"I've nothing more than a suspicion," Belle admitted. "But they're all part of the old Smethurst gang."

All through the conversation the young woman had been aware of Dusty's lack of participation. He had sat without speaking, a slight frown on his face, gazing down at his plate. However, she had known his behavior was not caused by a lack of interest. He was thinking about something, and she felt sure that the results of his summations would be worth hearing when they were delivered. At the name she mentioned, his eyes rose; but he still did not speak.

"What does that have to do with it?" the deputy challenged.

"Unless my information's wrong," Belle answered,

"Morbeus, using another name, served as a surgeon on Smethurst's staff during the war."

"Whooee!" the Kid breathed, thinking of various unproved rumors that had circulated regarding some of General Smethurst's inhuman treatment of Confederate soldiers who were prisoners of war. "Happen he was in on what they reckon happened in a couple of Smethurst's camps, those soft-shells might not have any choice but back his play. He could know too much about them."

"It could be," Belle conceded. "But, as I said, I've nothing more than suspicions to go on. One thing I do know. We pulled their teeth for a spell when we killed Smethurst,* but they've regained enough power to be a force to contend with in Washington. As long as they're backing Morbeus, there's no *legal* way of dealing with him."

"Which's why you sent word for us to join you," Mark guessed, having received a message the young woman had hired an out-of-work cowhand to deliver to the trail herd asking him to join her in Bannock's Ford.

"It is," Belle confirmed. "I've been out to scout the place a few times. There's a high wall all around the mission's buildings, so there's no way of seeing what's going on inside. Especially as you can't get close to the river's edge even without being seen by them. But I've got to know what he's got and is doing—and before the end of the month."

"Why then?" Mark asked.

"Because that's when he's going to sell whatever it is he stole," Belle explained. "And at least four countries are sending buyers to bid for it."

"Sounds like it's something real valuable," Tragg remarked.

"That's what's so puzzling," Belle replied. "I can't think of *anything* Haiti has to offer that would make France, Portugal, Spain, and Mexico send agents to try to buy it."

"Have you ever heard of voodoo, Belle?" Dusty put in.

* How this came about is told in THE HOODED RIDERS.—J.T.E.

"Voodoo?" the girl repeated, unable to think why such a question had been put. Yet she knew that it would not have been put unless there was a serious purpose and it was connected with the matter they were discussing. So she thought for a moment before going on. "I've heard colored folks talk about it. My old mammy back home used to tell the most scary stories to us. It's some kind of black magic. Witchcraft, spells and such things—"

"Damn it!" Tragg growled, glancing at the door of the dining room. "Gormley's come and he's headed this way."

CHAPTER ELEVEN

HE'LL SIC HIS *ZOMBIE* ON YOU

"Poor old Doctor Gollicker," Deputy Sheriff Jervis Tragg said, looking at the body that the Ysabel Kid had located after a display of track reading which had demonstrated how he had gained his reputation in that aspect of his duties as a scout. "Why in hell did that son of a bitch have to kill him this way?"

"Could be the poor bastard didn't know what he was doing," Dusty Fog suggested quietly, also turning away after glancing at the hideous ruin of the corpse's skull.

The arrival of Town Marshal Arthur Gormley had brought the discussion in the Jolene Hotel's dining room to an end. Much as Tragg and—he suspected—Belle Boyd would have liked to hear why Dusty Fog had expressed such an interest in voodoo, there was no opportunity for them to do so. It had been obvious that the municipal peace officer was deeply interested in what they meant to do, and none of them could think up a reason for dismissing him.

Showing the versatility that had made her famous as a Confederate spy and a capable secret agent, the girl had resumed the character of "Elvira Porterham." Watching Gormley, the deputy had been confident that he did not doubt the explanation of her presence and accepted she was only there in search of material for the book she claimed to be writing. Nothing about the marshal's attitude suggested that he suspected her true identity, or thought she was other than she pretended to be.

Having consumed their breakfasts while they were talking, the party had had no reason to remain in the dining room. So Tragg had suggested, as had been arranged the previous night, that the cowhands help him with the investigation of Gollicker's murder. Although Gormley's jurisdiction did not extend beyond the boundaries of Bannock's Ford, he had volunteered to go with them. As he was not usually so willing to offer his services, hoping to learn the reason for his untypical behavior, the deputy had raised no objections. However, his continued presence had prevented Belle from accompanying the posse. It also precluded a resumption of the conversation that he had interrupted.

Collecting Tarbrush and their horses from the livery barn, it having been considered inadvisable to leave the Negro in the town, the men had ridden to the clearing in which Gollicker had been killed. While the others kept back, the Kid had given the area a more thorough examination than was possible by moonlight. Despite the improved visibility he had stated that the conditions were not conducive to an extensive reading of the signs on the ground. Nevertheless, he had managed to guide them to where the body was hidden.

"That big nigger must've toted it here," Gormley suggested, before any of the others could respond to Dusty's statement.

"Looks that way," the Kid said blandly, although he knew this was not the case. He also did not ask why Gormley thought that the big Negro had gone away and waited until after Tarbrush had departed, then returned to carry off and hide the body. Instead, he continued, "Sure was a mean cuss, though. Smart too. He put the head into the water to wash away what was left of the blood 'n' such so's it wouldn't be spilled and mark the trail while he was toting the body off."

"Like you say, Lon," Mark Counter commented. "That was right smart thinking."

"Huh!" Gormley snorted, wanting to avert any subject that

121

might suggest somebody other than the dead Negro might be involved. Throwing a disdainful look to where Tarbrush was standing by the horses, he went on, "Niggers—"

"Would you-all say we're outside the town limits, Jervis?" the Kid asked, and something in his voice caused the marshal to stop speaking.

"Sure, Lon," the deputy confirmed, also noticing the change that had come over the Indian-dark Texan. "Why?"

"I've allus been taught not to mean-mouth a lawman in his own bailiwick," the Kid answered, sounding almost meek and mild. Then he swung toward the municipal peace officer. "Hombre. I'm part Comanch' and not ashamed who knows it. But I don't take kind to *anybody* tossing words like *half-breed* around in my hearing and I reckon Tarbrush here feels the same when he hears somebody keep saying 'nigger.' "

"Wh—?" the marshal spluttered, conscious of the way that—mild as the voice sounded—all the babyish innocence of the black-dressed Texan's face had been replaced by a coldly savage expression more suitable to a Comanche warrior.

"I go along with Lon on that, *Mr. Gormley,*" Mark stated, thumb-hooking his hands near the ivory butts of the Colt 1860 Army revolvers in the tied-down contoured holsters of his well-made *buscadero* gun belt.

"Wh—?" the peace officer repeated no more succinctly, aware that a Texas cowhand only used the honorific *mister* after having been introduced if he did not like the person he was addressing.

"So do I," Dusty declared, giving what was clearly the seal of approval to his companions' sentiments. "And, with that settled, I reckon Jervis wants to get on with what we're out here for."

"You figure on following that big n—hombre's sign and finding out where he went after he left here, Kid?" Gormley inquired in a placatory tone of voice, as the three men from the OD Connected began to turn away in a way that showed they considered the matter was closed.

"Happen that's what *Jervis* wants, I will," the Kid answered. "Only, seeing's we know where he went to from here, to a half-smart li'l ole Texas boy like me, it looks to make more sense was we to try to find out where he came *from.*"

"What good will that do?" Gormley asked, appreciating how such a discovery would not be to his advantage; especially as he was with the posse that would be making it. "He's dead'n' done for."

"Maybe there're some more like him where he came from," Dusty suggested, watching for how his words would be received by the marshal.

"There can't be!" Gormley almost yelped. Then, deciding that he had protested too quickly, he continued in a less vehement fashion, "Shucks, Cap'n Fog, you *saw* him. There *couldn't* be any more like him around, or somebody'd've mentioned seeing 'em."

"I'd have thought somebody would have mentioned seeing *him,* happen he'd been seen hereabouts," Dusty conceded, and the marshal could have bitten off his tongue for having aroused such a speculation. "Only, nobody has, have they, Jervis?"

"Not to *me,*" Tragg replied.

"That being so," Dusty went on, "I'll sleep a whole heap better when I know that there aren't any more of them around."

"And me," Tragg seconded. "Let's go and find out, Lon." His gaze flickered to the other peace officer and he continued, "Do you reckon it'll be all right for you-all to be away from the town while we're following the trail? It could take a fair spell."

Finding himself on the horns of a dilemma Gormley did not know what would be his best answer. From what he had seen so far, the Kid was sufficiently skillful to have no difficulty in following the Negro's back trail. Nor could the marshal think of any way of preventing this. So he was unable to decide whether he should accompany the posse, letting Professor Morbeus and Silkie Roelich know of his failure to divert them, or return to Bannock's Ford.

"It might be as well for you to keep an eye on things back there," Dusty prompted. "Some of those yahoos who were at the jailhouse last night could still be hankering for trouble. Besides, somebody has to make arrangements to have this body taken in for burial."

"Sure, Cap'n Fog, that's just what I was thinking," Gormley answered, relieved to have been offered two excellent reasons for returning. "So I'll go, unless you need me along, Jervis?"

"Shucks, no," Tragg replied. "Could be we'll be wasting our time. Like you-all said, there *couldn't* be any more like him around."

"I'll go back, then," Gormley declared.

"Now, there's a feller I could right easy take a dislike to," the Kid drawled, watching the municipal peace officer riding away. "And I don't mean just 'cause he wears a badge— although *that* helps. Damn it, he's disrespecting Grandpappy Long Walker's teaching. Any Pehnane *tuinep'** old enough to go hoss herding would've seen from the sign there was *three* fellers toting the body."

"Hot damn!" Tragg exclaimed, eyeing the Indian-dark Texan in well-simulated amazement. "I wondered whether *you'd* noticed that. I did, straight off, but I didn't want to belittle you by saying so."

"Now you-all can see why I don't cotton to badge-toting varmints," the Kid informed the other cowhands. "They're all sneaky 'n' underhanded—"

"Let's go find out where that hombre came from, shall we?" Dusty suggested, showing no sympathy for his amigo's comment.

"I was just going to say *that,"* the Kid objected. "Let's do it

* *Tuinep':* a pre-adolescent Comanche boy.—J.T.E.

124

'n' then we'll see how far this smart-alecky John Law can read sign."

However, on returning to the clearing, the deputy was not given an opportunity to display his prowess. Instead, despite commenting that "some folks did the work while the rest only talked," the Kid gave himself the responsibility of carrying out the task. Even without Tarbrush being present to advise him, he would have had no difficulty in finding the point at which the big Negro had emerged from the bushes. Nor did following the back track require the skill he had needed to locate Gollicker's body. The man had not made any attempt to conceal the evidence of his passing.

As a precaution against an ambush having been laid, Dusty followed close on the Kid's heels as they set off. Doing so allowed him to devote his full attention to the task and was a wise precaution. At first they passed through dense woodland that offered many places of concealment if somebody had wished to prevent searchers discovering where the Negro had come from.

Relieved of Gormley's unwanted presence Tragg was eager to resume the conversation that had been interrupted at the hotel. However, as the nature of the terrain compelled the party to ride in a single file, he had to wait until the trees and undergrowth grew less thickly before he could do so. Once the conditions permitted, he asked Mark to take over as lookout for the Kid.

"Why'd you-all ask Miss Boyd about voodoo?" the deputy inquired, after the change had been made and he was riding alongside the small Texan.

"It was what she said about how Morbeus might have been a surgeon under Smethurst in the war," Dusty replied. "There was a rumor that he'd had experiments carried out on prisoners by his medical staff, although nothing was ever proven."

"I mind hearing something like that," Tragg admitted. "Do you know what kind of experiments?"

"No," Dusty answered. "But Belle might."

"I still don't see how it's tied in with voodoo," Tragg stated.

"Likely it isn't," Dusty drawled. "Only, it made me think some about what Doc was telling us when she came in. You know, about that hombre Lon killed already being dead when he was shot."

"Oh, *that!*" the deputy barked, then looked to where the Wedge cowhand and Tarbrush were following closely enough to be able to hear what was being said. Although nothing showed on the former's pallid features, he realized that his comment could be misinterpreted and sought to make amends. "I'm not doubting's you-all know what you're doing with doctoring, Doc, but what you told us doesn't seem possible."

"I'm not denying *that*," the cowhand replied, showing no sign of being offended. "All I *know* is that the signs I saw pointed that way. Only, I'll go along with you-all, Jervis. I don't see how it ties up with that Morbeus hombre either."

"Could be it doesn't," Dusty conceded, glancing ahead to find out what was happening. As the Kid continued to ride at a steady pace, watched by Mark, he continued, "Only, I keep remembering why Belle told us she was sent down here."

"Because Morbeus wide-looped something the government in Haiti sets great store by," Tragg drawled. "But how does that—?"

"I read something about voodoo in a book one time," Dusty explained. "According to the writer, it's practised a whole lot in Haiti. Even the president and the government use it to keep the people under control, or so he claimed."

"Aw, hell, Dusty!" the deputy protested. "Miss Boyd allowed's it was nothing more than some kind of witchcraft mumbo-jumbo—"

"Don't sell witchcraft short, Jervis," Doc warned. "I've heard tell of how Negro conjure-women and hex-throwers put out death curses and they do say, happen whoever gets the curse put on 'em believes in it, that old curse'll work."

"They sure enough do work!" the young Negro put in,

with complete and earnest conviction. "My old Auntie Mandy-Mae done got a double-whammy hex put on her, which's the worse kind to get hit by. And, though she'd never had so much's a day's illness in all her life, she was's dead's a butchered shoat* afore a week went by. There wasn't *nothing* to show how she died."

"What do you-all know about voodoo, amigo?" Dusty inquired, remembering that the author had claimed it was also practised by colored people in the southern United States.

"Nothing much, 'cepting li'l bits's kinfolk from down Louisiana way told," Tarbrush replied, and went on with vehemence. "Which they didn't say much and I wasn't wanting to find out, seeing's they reckoned them voodoo doctors can bring a dead feller back to life 'n' make him do things. That's something I don't want no part of."

"That's another thing the writer said," Dusty drawled soberly. "He reckoned that the voodoo priests in Haiti turn corpses into something called—"

"Zombies's what my kin allowed they was called," Tarbrush supplied, when the small Texan paused and threw an interrogative glance in his direction. "Way they tell it, happen you-all riles up a voodoo-doctor, or if somebody's don't like you pays him to, he'll sic his zombie on you, and seeing's it's already dead, there ain't no way you can stop it when it comes at you."

"Aw, come on, now, Dusty!" Tragg said, suddenly understanding the way in which the conversation was progressing. "Are you telling me's you-all reckon that hombre the Kid downed was one of them zombies?"

"I'm just telling you what I got to thinking about," Dusty corrected. "No matter what way you-all look at it, there was *something* mighty peculiar about him. For one thing, I kicked him in the balls hard enough to put even a man his size down, but he never showed he as much as felt it."

"That's as may be," Tragg answered. "But Tarbrush just

* Shoat: a young pig.—J.T.E.

127

now reckoned's there's no way you can kill a zombie, and you-all sure enough brought that hombre in dead."

"Lon killed him, all right," Dusty admitted, and looked over his shoulder. "Could he have taken some kind of drug that stopped him feeling pain, Doc?"

"He *could* have, and what you said about the way his eyes had a glassy stare, I thought that's what it must be," the cowhand replied. "Only, I've never heard of one so potent it'd stand off the kind of pain he should've felt the way you kicked him. One of his balls had burst open. So, if there is such a drug, I'd reckon it'd be way too powerful for him to have been able to keep walking even, much less do all he did. And, even if he was drugged—"

"That doesn't explain what you found when you-all opened him up this morning," the deputy concluded, guessing correctly what Doc had intended to say next. "Or would a drug like that make his insides go the way they had?"

"The Good Lord only knows," the cowhand replied. "I've never heard of any such drug, so I wouldn't even want to guess what effect it'd have if there was one."

"Aw, hell!" Tragg said, slapping at his left thigh in a frustrated manner. "It just isn't possible!"

"A few years back most folks were saying the same about doctors being able to put patients to sleep so they could be cut open and operated on without feeling it," Doc pointed out. "But it's being done now."

"I mean about zombies," the deputy corrected. "There's just no such thing. It's like that loup-garou* critter folks down to Louisiana tell scary stories about. You know, the one's they reckon can change from a man to a wolf and back. They're nothing more than tall tales to frighten folks and give 'em a thrill."

"I remember one thing about the loup-garou stories, though," Dusty put in quietly. "There's one way you-all can kill it. Shoot it with a silver bullet."

* The loup-garou is more generally known as a "werewolf."

"I've heard that too," Doc admitted, sounding puzzled and wondering what the small Texan had in mind while guiding the conversation along such unusual lines.

"Blast it all!" Tragg barked, sharing the cowhand's puzzlement and, although he doubted that such could be the explanation, considering the possibility that he was being made the victim of a practical joke. "Are you pair telling me that the Kid had a *silver* bullet in his yellowboy* last night?"

"Nope," Dusty contradicted. "Just plain lead. But the thing is, in the stories, there's a way the loup-garou can be killed." Once more he glanced to the rear, asking, "How about with a zombie, Tarbrush?"

"I've never heard tell of *nothing's* can kill one," the Negro answered. "They do say's how a zombie can't eat nothing that's got salt on it, but I never heard of one being killed by it. Anyways, seeing's it's dead already, don't seem natural's it could be killed over again."

"Looks like that hombre couldn't be a zombie, then, Dusty," Tragg declared, and let out a humorless laugh. "I'll be damned if you haven't nearly got me thinking he could have been."

"How about vampires?" Dusty inquired in a neutral tone.

"Vampires?" the deputy repeated.

"Not those damned bats that sometimes come up from Mexico," Dusty elaborated. "I mean the jaspers who can turn themselves into bats and go around killing folks to drink the blood. According to the stories the vampire's already dead. But you-all can make wolf-bait of him a second time and for keeps by driving a wooden stake through his heart, or stopping him from getting back into his coffin afore sunup."

"They do say dropping him into running water'll do it too," Doc continued, beginning to see what Dusty was leading up to.

"Don't look like it'd be all that hard to kill off a vampire,

* The brass frame of the Winchester Model of 1866 rifle, or carbine, was responsible for the name "yellowboy."—J.T.E.

then," Tragg commented dryly, sharing the slender cow-hand's growing understanding. "For what it means."

"Both the loup-garou and the vampire are told about as having supernatural powers," Dusty went on. "But that doesn't mean there's no way they can be killed."

"I'll give you that," the deputy said. "But them things don't exist outside a few scary stories."

Jervis Tragg was a very competent peace officer and belonged to a family that had been—and would continue to be*—prominent in the enforcement of Texas laws for many years. However, while he had been trained to cope with all the normal legal infringements that came his way, the conversation in which he was participating had reached a dimension far beyond anything he had so far experienced. A hard-bitten realist taught to accept nothing other than provable facts, he was skeptical where such mentions of supernatural phenomenon were concerned. So, although he was finding the conversation an interesting diversion that helped to pass the time while waiting for something more purposeful and practical to happen, he could not see that anything useful could come of it.

"One thing's for sure," the deputy told himself as he waited for Dusty's answer to his statement, "—there's no such thing as a zombie, and no matter what else that hombre they toted in might be, he couldn't be one."

However, the small Texan's answer did not come. Even as he was about to reply, he and Tragg noticed that the Kid and Mark were coming to a halt. The deputy realized that they were very close to the edge of the woodland. Ahead of them lay the lakelike portion of the Rio Grande upon which the Island Mission was situated.

* Some details of a current member of the Tragg family's participation in the law enforcement of Texas are given in the author's Rockabye County series of books.—J.T.E.

CHAPTER TWELVE

DO ANY OF THEM KNOW *US*?

"Whee-doggie!" the Ysabel Kid exclaimed sotto voce, although there was no immediate necessity for such a precaution. "I'll tell you-all that Belle wasn't just whistling 'Dixie' when she allowed's she couldn't find a way of getting close to that place without being seen."

Standing at the Indian-dark Texan's right side, sharing the concealment offered by one of the last trees before the woodland ended, Dusty Fog nodded in agreement with the sentiment. However, he did not lower the pair of field glasses that he had taken from his saddlebags and continued with his examination of the Island Mission and its surroundings.

While the tracks that the Kid had been following were still continuing, on learning that the posse was approaching the area in which Belle Boyde was interested, the small Texan had asked Deputy Sheriff Jervis Tragg if they could reconnoiter before allowing themselves to be seen crossing the open ground that lay ahead. Appreciating the wisdom of the suggestion the peace officer had concurred. So, leaving their horses in Tarbrush's care, the rest of the men had moved forward on foot. Each of them had found himself a place of concealment from which he could conduct his observations. From what they saw, none of them felt that the Rebel Spy was in error with her summation of the situation.

Beyond the points at which it emerged from and reentered areas of woodland, the Rio Grande spread out to fill a circular depression something over a mile in circumference. The terrain on both sides all around the edges of the Mission Lake, as the section was sometimes called, was completely devoid of trees and bushes. In fact, there was no cover of any size on the open ground to offer the means of an unobserved approach.

The mission itself had been erected on a low and roughly egg-and-saucer-shaped piece of bare, rocky ground that rose in the center of the river. However, it was surrounded by a high adobe* wall and, as the gates were closed, only the roof of the main building was visible from where the posse were standing. Nor, according to Doc Leroy—who was making the experiment—was it possible to see what went on beyond the wall even from up in the branches of a tree. A series of metal tripods, each surmounted by an iron basket and with a woodpile near it, were positioned at regular intervals around as much of the island as could be seen.

Access to the property was attained either by the two rowing boats that were drawn up on the shore, a canoe, or a steam launch, which—apart from having its armament removed—was similar to those employed by Lieutenant William Barker Cushing, U.S.N., to carry out his successful raid on the Confederate warship *Albemarle*† and used less effectively by another northern naval officer during an incident in which Dusty had been involved.‡ The latter pair of vessels were moored to a wooden landing stage, which extended in the direction of the northern bank of the river,

* Adobe: a building material made from sun-dried, calcareous clay formed into bricks or applied to a wooden framework in the form of a plaster. —J.T.E.

† Lieutenant William B. Cushing led a flotilla of seven launches. Each was armed with twelve-pounder boat-howitzer, but attacked with a "spar torpedo," an explosive charge carried on the end of a fourteen-foot pole that could be raised and lowered as required. The charge was detonated by a lanyard connected to a friction primer, a description of which is given in THE HOODED RIDERS. The raid took place on the Roanoke River, North Carolina, on October 27, 1864. The *Albermarle* was a large battle-ram, a metal warship with a reinforced bow, used to crash into and sink other vessels.—J.T.E.

‡ Told in THE COLT AND THE SABER.—J.T.E.

where another stage offered a point at which to come ashore.

By the landing stage on the Texas bank were two fair-sized, and one smaller, adobe buildings. All appeared to have been erected recently. Several horses, some of which were clearly only suitable for draft purposes, were moving around in a large pole corral beyond the buildings. A buggy and a small covered wagon were parked under the lean-tos of the larger structures, but there was no sign of their occupants.

"What do you make of it, Dusty?" Tragg inquired, from his position behind a nearby clump of bushes.

"Nothing I like the look of," the small Texan replied, lowering the field glasses. "I reckon those cressets* go all the way around the mission?"

"Miffin Kennedy and Dick King got the fathers at the mission to let them set one up on each side of the island as beacons for their boats," the deputy explained. "But Morbeus added the rest when he took over. I haven't been across the river to look, but I don't reckon he left out that side."

"It's not likely he would have," Dusty admitted. "And, once they're lit, I'd say there's no way anybody could land on the island without being seen. What do you reckon, Lon?"

"It'd be harder'n hell," the Kid concluded, having been studying the island with a keen, experienced—if unaided—gaze. "Happen you could get a boat close enough for you to swim in, there's just one place you *might* be able to sneak through. Between them two boats. Only, they'll most likely have a guard there. Mind you, I don't have no fancy white man's doohickey to look through, so I can't be certain sure."

"These've got 'Give Them Back' on them," Dusty warned, handing the field glasses to his amigo and, ignoring a com-

---

* Cresset: a receptacle made of an inflammable material that was filled with a fire and used for the purposes of illumination.—J.T.E.

ment of "danged Injun-giver" from him, addressed the peace officer. "How many men do they have, Jervis?"

"I don't know for sure," Tragg replied. "But when Miffin Kennedy brought Morbeus and some gear up on the *Ranchero II*, he allowed's there was at least ten hired guns and the peons from below the border who was setting up the place. Another four came through town, riding shotgun on that wagon when it arrived. The peons have all gone now, but the *pistoleros* are still around. I couldn't say whether there're more or less of them, though. They're not like you blasted cowhands and all come in together a-whooping and hollering on pay night."

"Us blasted cowhands help pay you John Laws' wages," the Kid pointed out, taking the field glasses from his eyes. "Which I'll never know why we let 'em use our hard-earned tax money for fool things like that." Then he became serious and reported, "There're some fellers in those houses by the river, Dusty, but I don't know how many. Thing being, even if you-all could figure on taking them out quietly, that mission's built like a fort."

"And even if they decide against making a fight for it, we wouldn't be a whole heap better off," Dusty went on. "Before we could reach them, they'd be in that steam launch and headed off as fast's its engines can carry them."

"If the engines were fired up and ready," Tragg pointed out.

"I don't think a feller who takes so many other precautions would overlook *that* one," Dusty drawled. "Fact being, I'd be willing to bet a couple of dollars that the engine's kept fired up ready for use all through the night."

"I'd take you, only I know you only offer to put up money on 'certains,'" the Kid declared. "And here's your blasted glasses, afore I get asked for 'em. Fool things wasn't worth a cuss, anyways. All they told me was what I'd *already* figured. I knowed Belle wouldn't't've needed to ask for *our* help unless things were extra tough, but I hadn't reckoned they'd be *this* bad. Hey, though, Dusty, didn't you-all have to tackle a place something like this up to Arkansas in the war?"

"Yes," the small Texan agreed. "Only that time, I had me a damned great Parrot rifle* to help me."

"You-all figure it'll come to taking them, Dusty?" Tragg asked, having heard of the incident to which the Kid was referring.†

"It'll likely have to be done," the small Texan replied. "Belle's damned good at her work and the man she works under's nobody's fool. So, happen they feel that Morbeus has to be stopped selling whatever it was he wide-looped from Haiti, it has to be *real* important. In which case the only way to stop him is by taking the mission and making sure he isn't able to."

"I'll do anything I can to help, you and Sheriff Trimble'll back me up on it," Tragg promised, impressed by the solemnity with which Dusty's words had been uttered. "So to hell with those letters's Morbeus showed us, no matter who signed them in Washington and Mexico City both."

"*Gracias, amigo,*" the small Texan responded, pleased with the compliment implied by such an unhesitating offer of support. "How do you-all feel about us making a start at it by going down there and having a talk with him?"

"Are you figuring on taking him *now?*" the deputy asked, sounding startled.

"Nope," Dusty answered. "Just having a talk with him."

"We can try," Tragg said doubtfully. "Only, we don't have any *legal* right to make him take us out to the mission, and even after losing Hooper last night, he's pretty near certain to have us outnumbered."

"I haven't forgotten *that,*" Dusty assured the deputy with a grin. "And, seeing's how we're all—" he paused, looking pointedly at the Kid and then amended, "Well, most all of us, anyways, are honest, upright, and law-abiding citizens, we

---

* Used in this context, the word *rifle* means a cannon with a rifled barrel. —J.T.E.

† Told in THE BIG GUN.—J.T.E.

wouldn't want you-all to do *anything* unless it was right and legal. Let's go, happen you've seen all you want to, Jervis."

"What've you-all got in that tricky li'l ole Rio Hondo mind, amigo?" asked the Kid, as the men—including Doc, who had descended from his point of vantage—started to retreat in the direction of their horses.

"I was wondering that too," Tragg went on, studying the small Texan's impassive features and trying to work out what lay behind the soft, all too casual sounding words.

"You're a duly appointed and sworn-in deputy sheriff of Kinney County, which we're still in, and on the trail of a mighty dangerous murderer," Dusty explained. "So I'd say's it's more than just your right, it's your solemn duty to ask questions of *anybody* if you reckon they might know something that could help you find him. Particularly when he might still be lurking around and endangering lives."

"That's be my right and duty, all right, but for one little bitty thing," Tragg conceded. "Could be that Roelich was still in town and knows's you brought that jasper in dead last night. Happen he does, he'll have told Morbeus about it— always assuming's that jasper came from the mission, that is."

"Why, sure, I'm not denying you've hit the target," Dusty drawled. "Only, they can't tell us they know he's dead. Not without showing us that he did come from the mission. So, was *I* leading this posse, I'd say we should drift down there and find out what they have to tell us."

"I've always heard tell that great minds think alike," Tragg stated, accepting his horse's reins from Tarbrush. "And, see-ing's *I'm* leading thishere posse, I conclude we should drift down there and find out what they have to tell us."

"I wouldn't want to go raising difficulties," Mark Counter put in, swinging astride his magnificent seventeen-hand blood-bay stallion. "But mightn't they think it's just a li'l mite peculiar that we're trailing that hombre this way?"

"They might," Tragg admitted, also mounting his horse. "But can I be blamed if the county don't give me enough

136

expense money to hire a tracker who knows when he's on a back trail and's brought us here?"

"Do I get *paid?*" the Kid inquired hopefully, boarding his big white with a deft swing and sliding the Winchester rifle from his saddle boot.

"Any money that's coming is turned over to your employer," Dusty answered, settling on his saddle, "or to his representative on the scene, which's me."

"Either way," drawled the Kid, "it comes out's *I* don't get paid."

"The county wouldn't want me to pay *anybody* who doesn't know a back from a forward trail," the deputy pointed out, knowing that the conversation was not serious. "Let's get moving."

"You-all want me to stick to this here trail's my employer, or his blasted representative on the scene, won't get paid for me following?" the Kid wanted to know.

"I'd say so," Dusty supplied, losing his levity when the peace officer glanced in his direction. "No matter where that hombre came out of the water, we'll have an excuse to go along and talk to Morbeus."

Setting off in a similar formation to that which they had adopted until halting, the posse rode from the trees. The Kid led them along the now barely discernible tracks left by the big Negro, which took them to the edge of the river some distance from the landing stage. Once there, they halted and gathered for the kind of conference that might have developed if they had not anticipated such a development. Then Tragg pointed to the buildings and, fanning out instead of remaining in two files, they made their way in that direction.

Although there had been no sign of the occupants up to that point, they began to make their appearance as the posse was approaching. Five men came out of the largest of the buildings and four more emerged from the second. Clad in the fashion of cowhands, townsmen, or professional gamblers, they all had one thing in common. Each had at least one revolver visible on his person. Furthermore, the majority had tied the tips of their holsters to their thighs as an aid to making a faster draw. However, Silkie Roelich was not with them. Nor did any of them have weapons in their hands. Despite the diversity of their costume nothing about them led Dusty and his companions to assume they were other than hired guns.

"Do any of you recognize any of them?" the small Texan inquired, while the posse was still beyond audible distance.

"I don't know any of 'em," the Kid declared. "But I sure's hell know *what* they are—and I don't cotton to it."

"Thing being, do any of them know *us?*" Dusty drawled, after the rest of the party had disclaimed knowledge. "Happen they don't, they might make some fool mistake like trying to scare us off. Now, we wouldn't want *that* to happen, would we?"

"We surely wouldn't," Mark agreed piously. "Why, *somebody* could get hurt was that to happen."

"Wouldn't *none* of us want that, for shame," the Kid went on, looking and sounding as innocent as a church pew filled with choirboys singing for the bishop.

Which did not fool a man who knew the Indian-dark Texan as well as Doc Leroy did. Glancing from one to another of the OD Connected riders, he turned his gaze to Tragg and said, "Do you-all get the feeling that somebody knows something that we don't?"

"I get the feeling that somebody knows something I'd rather *not* know about until *after* it's happened," the peace officer replied.

Studying the men from the buildings through range-wise eyes, Dusty formed conclusions about them. While all undoubtedly earned their wages by selling their guns, he did not consider any of them to be top grade *pistoleros*. However, in Roelich's absence, it was easy to pick out those who regarded themselves as the leaders. Three in number, they advanced a short distance ahead of their companions. At the right was a tall, lean young man in dandified cowhand clothes, who toted two low-tied Colts and bore a family resemblance by being Toby Hooper's cousin Si. Almost as tall, slightly heavier in build and older, the next of the trio also dressed range style and belted two guns. He was not so tidy, having a stubble of beard and longish hair. Wearing the attire of a gambler the last man was smaller and lighter, with a Remington Army revolver tucked butt forward on the left side of the silk sash around his waist.

"Mind holding the hosses again, Tarbrush?" Tragg inquired, as his party came to a halt and dismounted some fifty yards from the hardcases.

"Nope," the young Negro replied, knowing that his presence with the posse might be used by the men from the buildings as a means of provoking trouble.

"Howdy," greeted the deputy, walking at the head of the other Texans and speaking when there was around thirty feet between the two groups.

"You wanting something?" demanded the member of the leading trio who wore the garb of a gambler.

"To see Professor Morbeus," Tragg replied, still advancing at a leisurely gait.

"Could be he'll not want to see *you-all*," Si Hooper answered.

"Then we'll likely have to *make* him!" Dusty announced, before the deputy could respond to what was clearly a challenge.

Although they had only met for the first time the previous night, Tragg was able to detect a change in the small Texan's voice and, as a glance informed him, attitude. The tone and now swaggering walk was that of one who wanted to convince others he was tough.

Clearly Hooper drew such a conclusion. If any other member of the posse had made the remark, particularly as they were now almost with reaching distance, he might have overlooked it. However, to hear it spoken by a small and insignificant-looking person, whom he assumed to be either a wrangler or cook's louse and not even a cowhand, aroused his bullying nature.

"Try it!" Hooper challenged and, meaning to cow the small man and impress the other newcomers with his speed on the draw, sent his right hand dipping to the butt of the offside Colt.

Instantly, as far as the young hardcase was concerned, Dusty appeared to go through an amazing metamorphosis. He seemed to take on size until it was Hooper who felt dwarfed by comparison. The sensation was both unnerving and flustering.

While Hooper's draw was fairly fast, Dusty was acting with even greater rapidity. Two strides carried him close enough for what he planned, which was *not* to pull either of his Colts.

Whipping across, the small Texan's left hand cupped over and grasped the cylinder of Hooper's Colt as it was lifting into alignment. At almost the same instant his right caught the barrel from underneath. Completely unprepared for such a response, or Dusty's unexpected strength, the hardcase could not prevent the muzzle of his weapon being turned inward. His thumb lost its grip on the hammer, which just reached the fully cocked position, but he had sufficient sense to relax the forefinger's pressure on the trigger. The Colt did not fire, but his troubles were far from over. Still working in smooth coordination Dusty's right fist twisted the weapon from its owner's grasp and the left transferred to the now empty hand with fingers on its palm and the thumb pointing upward at the back. Having completed the two moves practically simultaneously, he applied a pressure that bent Hooper's hand upward and put considerable pain on its wrist.

Knowing Dusty, Mark had been expecting something to happen. Even as his amigo went into action, he sprang forward with almost equal speed. He selected the short gambler as the object of his attentions. Catching the startled man by the throat and sash before he recovered his wits, the blond giant lifted. Showing no more apparent strain than if he had been handling a baby, he hoisted the man above

140

his head. Then, with a surging heave, he flung his captive at the group of hired guns.

Equally aware that Dusty was planning something, the Kid flipped the Winchester to his shoulder. He had noticed the barrel of a rifle protruding from the open door of the second building and was aware of what the sight portended. So he was ready to deal with the concealed wielder of the weapon. Hearing the commotion the other stepped into view and very soon had cause to wish he had not. Flame erupted from the muzzle of the Kid's repeater. Not just once, but three times in a second and a half, as taking advantage of its smoothly functioning mechanism,* he worked the lever to eject the spent cases and replenished the chamber with live rounds. Nor were they wild shots, but each flew where it was intended. The rifle was torn from the hired gun's grasp with the first bullet and hit twice more as it was leaving.

Being acquainted with the small Texan, Doc had anticipated the possibility of action. So, remembering the exchange of comments between the OD Connected trio and the Wedge cowhand's remark as they were walking from the horses, had Tragg. Demonstrating his exceptional speed Doc flashed the ivory-handled Colt from its holster, and although somewhat slower, the deputy duplicated his movement. However, even as their weapons were pointing in the required direction, the gambler thrown by Mark crashed among the main body of hired guns and prevented any concerted resistance.

That the blond giant had picked the gambler as his objective was further proof of how well he knew, and the faith he had in, Dusty.

Still retaining the agonizing grip on Hooper's hand, the small Texan saw the remaining member of the trio belatedly

---

* An advertisement put out by the Great Western Gun Works announced with regard to the Winchester Model of 1866, otherwise known as the "Improved Henry," "They can be fired *seventeen times* without reloading, at the rate of *two shots per second.*"—J.T.E.

attempting to participate. Even as the man's hand went to the butt of his gun, Dusty swung what a student of karate would have identified as a *mawashi geri* roundhouse kick. Its recipient might not have known its Japanese name, but he could—and later did with considerable profanity—testify to how effective such an attack was. Taking the blow by the small Texan's right boot, all the air was slammed from his lungs. The thought of completing his draw ended as, folding like a closing jackknife, he stumbled back and collapsed to his knees.

Squealing in pain, Hooper scrabbled with his free hand for the second Colt. It proved to be a mistake. Having rendered his companion hors de combat, Dusty swung and slammed the butt of the captured weapon against the side of his jaw. For a moment bright lights burst inside his head. Then all went black and he toppled unconscious to the ground.

"Anybody who acts hostile gets shot for resisting the law!" Tragg warned, lining his Colt as Hooper was landing.

The information and possibility of having it carried out was enhanced by Dusty and Mark each producing his brace of Colts at a pace matched only by the move Doc had already made. Nor did the fact that the Kid's rifle was still held ready for use go unnoticed by the discomforted hired guns. Even those who had not been entangled by the gambler's flying body realized that it would be fatally foolish to ignore the deputy's comment.

"I told you-all's they mightn't recognize us, Dusty, Mark," the Kid declared in aggrieved tones, seeing a way in which to help Tragg make his point.

"That you did, *Kid,*" the small Texan agreed, although he no longer seemed diminutive to the hired guns, duplicating his amigo's line of reasoning.

"*Dusty! Mark! Kid!*" croaked one of the men who had avoided being hit by the blond giant's human missile. "You —you—you're Dusty Fog, Mark Counter, and the Ysabel Kid!"

142

"We knew that all the time," Dusty drawled, as startled exclamations rose from the other hired guns. "Now you-all'd best tend to those two and get word to the professor that we aim to make talk with him."

"What's going on there?" yelled a voice from beyond the buildings.

Looking in the speaker's direction the small Texan discovered that it would be unnecessary to send the message. Tragg had described Morbeus, and although he was dressed in a different fashion, Dusty decided he was one of the men in the canoe that had stopped some distance from the shore. Further information supplied by the deputy suggested the other was Silkie Roelich.

"Looks like we don't have to worry no more," the Kid remarked quietly, having made the same identification. "We'll be able to take him now."

"Like hell we will," Dusty replied. "He's not intending to come any closer until he figures it's safe. And he's smart enough to have somebody out there to back him up, or at least to get rid of whatever it is that Belle's after."

"How do you want to play it, Dusty?" Tragg inquired, agreeing with the summation.

"Let him come ashore," the small Texan answered. "Tell him the truth about why we're here and see what he says. One thing's for sure. We're not going to get whatever he's got out there this easily."

143

CHAPTER THIRTEEN

YOU'LL NOT SET ME AFOOT

"No, sheriff, I have never seen such a man as you describe," Professor Hogreth Morbeus said emphatically, his accent New England. "Nor do I employ any Negroes. I'm afraid you'll have to take my word for that. You can't go out and search the mission."

The owner of the Island Mission was tall, heavily built, in his early fifties, and had a mane of longish white hair. Apart from his light blue eyes, which were hard, he had hearty sun-reddened features that displayed no suggestion of academic leanings. Nor did his attire. He was in his shirtsleeves, with neither tie nor collar. He had on yellowish-brown nankeen trousers and rawhide moccasins, but did not appear to be armed.

On landing and being introduced by Deputy Sheriff Jervis Tragg to the other members of the posse, Morbeus had told how he and Silkie Roelich had seen them coming, so set off to meet them. Learning what had happened, he ordered his boss gun to fire the three men who had caused the disturbance. Then he had listened while the deputy explained the posse's presence and requested information.

"Do you mind if I ask why not, sir?" Dusty Fog inquired politely.

"It's for your own good," Morbeus replied. "If I can speak with you and the sheriff privately, Captain Fog, I will explain."

"Sure," Tragg assented, when the small Texan glanced at

him. "The point is, gentlemen," Morbeus announced, after he had accompanied the two men beyond the hearing of the others (the posse had holstered their weapons before he landed and stood a short distance away from his employees), "my purpose for being here and the reason I have been given the letters of introduction that I showed to you on your previous visit, Sheriff, is that I've been hired by Congress and the Mexican government to try to find a cure for anthrax.* And I'm sure I don't need to tell *anybody* who has *your* connections with the ranching business what the successful outcome of my work will mean, Captain Fog?"

"By the Good Lord, you don't!" Dusty agreed, with the kind of vehemence he felt such a statement warranted. "Once that takes hold, it'll wipe out every head of cattle and stays around for long after they're dead and rotted away."

"And it won't only be the cattle that are affected either," Morbeus pointed out. "Human beings can catch and carry it to others too."

"Damn it!" Tragg said, wondering if a mistake had been made by Belle Boyd. "Why didn't you tell the sheriff and me about this when we came out?"

"For the same reason that I didn't want any of those men there to learn of it," Morbeus explained. "If people found out that I am working with animals infected by, or that have died from, anthrax, there would be panic and they might try to drive me away from an ideal location for my experiments. Only Mr. Roelich and my assistant know what I'm doing. The rest of the men are hired for my protection, to ensure my privacy and as a protection against either white outlaws or Mexican bandidos who might think I have something of value on the island. So I must ask you both to give me your word as gentlemen not to tell *anyone* else."

"Well, I dunno about that," Tragg said, sounding doubtful.

---

* Anthrax: a highly infectious and malignant febrile disease caused by the microorganism *Bacillus anthracis*. The nature of the causative agent was demonstrated by C. J. Davane in 1863.—J.T.E.

"I don't reckon's the sheriff'd be any too took with the notion of you-all bringing anthrax into Kinney County."

"I assure you that, with the precautions I take, there is *no* chance of *that* happening," Morbeus declared, darting a look which implied, *What did I tell you?* at the small Texan. "None of my guards ever enter the mission and every stitch of clothing that is used inside stays there, which is why I'm dressed so informally."

"You have *my* word, sir," Dusty announced firmly, and threw a frown that seemed pregnant with threat at the deputy. "And, with something *this* important to ranching, General Hardin and the Cattlemen's Association will back you to the hilt should *anybody* interfere."

"That's most gratifying to know, sir," Morbeus boomed. "How about you, *Deputy?*"

"Sure," Tragg conceded, somewhat hesitantly. "If General Hardin and the Cattlemen's Association're for it, I reckon it'll be all right."

"It will," Morbeus assured the peace officer. "You say that the Negro's tracks came from the river down there?"

"Yes," Dusty confirmed, then turned his attention to the deputy. "It'll be like *I* said. He was wearing broken shackles. So he must've escaped from a chain gang down in Mexico and run for the border."

"Sure," Tragg admitted. "Which being so, we might's well head back to town. If the fellers who're running the chain gang come, I'll tell them what's happened."

"What do you think, Mr. Roelich?" Professor Morbeus asked, describing the conversation as he watched the posse riding away. "Have they taken my story?"

"If Fog has, Tragg'll go along with it," the boss gun answered. "No small-town peace officer's wants to keep holding his badge's going to cross Ole Devil Hardin and the Cattlemen's Association. Do you-all still want me to fire those three?"

"Give them some money and tell them to go upriver

146

somewhere for a couple of weeks, then come back," Morbeus ordered. "By the time they do, we'll have finished and gone. The damned fools could have caused more attention than we can stand."

"Young Hooper won't be any use for a spell," Roelich drawled unsympathetically, sharing his employer's sentiments. "His jaw's bust. But with them gone and the other Hooper kid dead, I'd best go into Bannock's Ford tomorrow and see if I can get a few men to replace them."

"That would be the best idea," Morbeus praised, then he grinned. "Well, I may as well go back to the mission and see if I can learn the cure for anthrax as I told Fog I would."

However, if the two men had been able to hear the discussion that was taking place between the members of the departing posse, neither would have felt so smug and self-satisfied over their "success."

"So he's looking for a cure for anthrax," Tragg drawled, as his party were riding along the river trail. "What do you-all make of *that*, Dusty?"

"I might have believed him, but for one thing," the small Texan replied. "Those soft-shells who've signed his letter of introduction aren't likely to have backed something that could help the cattle business. Too many of us southrons are getting rich and influential through it for *them* to want that. On top of which, if they were behind something that important, even if they tried to hide it, Belle and her boss would have heard."

"That was *two* things," the Kid pointed out.

"Do you reckon whatever he wide-looped from Haiti could help cure anthrax?" Mark Counter asked, having been told of the "private" information. "If he had, it'd be worth plenty to any country. Especially one that raises a lot of beef."

"It could be," Dusty admitted. "Or he thought fast and came up with a damned smart reason for stopping us going to the Mission. Nobody with a lick of good sense would go near a place that might have anthrax in it."

"How's that take in you pair?" asked the Kid, looking from the small Texan to the peace officer. "I've never knowed you to show even a lick of it."

"Anyways," Dusty went on, ignoring the remark, "I'll be right interested to hear what Belle thinks about it."

However, on the posse's return to Bannock's Ford, the small Texan was not given the opportunity to consult with the Rebel Spy. Before they could even dismount at the livery barn, its owner came out to deliver some disturbing news.

"One of your trail hands's just now rid in, Cap'n Fog. He was looking for Mark here and a doctor."

"Where's he now?" Dusty demanded, without asking for further details.

"I told him's you'd all rid out with Jervis 'n's the doctor's been killed," the owner replied. "So he allowed he'd go get a meal at the Man on the Wall and then, happen you wasn't back when he'd finished, he'd go look for you."

"Let's go!" Dusty ordered, and this time he did not wait for instructions from the deputy.

There was a large crowd in the Man on the Wall Saloon when the posse entered. A leathery-faced old cowhand rose from his table and hurried to greet them.

"We ran into some fuss, Cap'n Fog," the elderly man announced, and sensing that something of interest might be in the air, the rest of the customers fell silent to listen. "Bandidos jumped us, put lead into a couple of the boys, 'n' got away with maybe a hundred head. If it hadn't been for Waco—."

"What!" Dusty thundered furiously. "So that blasted no-account bone idle young son of a bitch I let Clay Allison talk me into taking on's to blame for it, is he?"

"Y-you might say that," answered the old-timer, falling back a pace and looking aghast before the small Texan's wrath.

"God damn it!" Dusty went on, just as heatedly. "I *knew* I should never have hired him. Go to the herd, Mark, and take Doc with you, if he can be spared by the Wedge."

"Sure, Dusty," the blond giant replied, and the Wedge cowhand gave his concurrence.

"And, Mark!" Dusty continued, as the two men made as if to turn away. "When you get there, tell that no-good bastard to stay well clear of *me!*"

After many years at such work the senior of the three bartenders behind the counter of the Man on the Wall Saloon felt that he was a shrewd judge of character. Studying the youngster who was crossing the barroom shortly after nine o'clock in the evening, he drew conclusions that he felt sure were accurate. He also considered that it would be ill advised to air them verbally.

Six feet in height, with a powerful figure that had not yet attained full manhood, the newcomer was a handsome—if surly and truculent looking—blond cowhand. He walked with an arrogant swagger, hands never far from the staghorn butts of the Colt 1860 Army revolvers in the tied-down holsters of his excellently made gun belt.

"Whiskey," the youngster demanded rather than requested, tossing down a silver dollar. "And make sure you-all fill that glass right up."

"I allus do *that,*" the bartender replied, wondering where he had last seen the newcomer.

"And *I've* met some's needed reminding to," the blond countered.

Deciding that his latest customer was either on the prod, or just naturally ornery and truculent, the bartender did not respond to the comment. While tough and capable of defending himself under most conditions, his instincts warned that—young though the cowhand undoubtedly was—he had better avoid trouble. The two Army Colts hung just right and he sensed that their wearer was more than ready, willing, and *very* able to use them.

"Waco, honey!" called a female voice, and much to the bartender's relief, it diverted the youngster's attention.

Hurrying forward to throw her arms around the cowhand's neck and kiss him, the speaker was a girl who had only arrived and been hired by the owner that afternoon. She was something of an enigma to the bartender. In her late twenties, about five feet seven inches tall, she was beautiful under her makeup. While slender, the figure inside the cheap, shiny red dress was good and her black stocking-covered legs were muscled like a dancer's. However, the way in which her blond hair had been cut boyishly short suggested that she had recently served a term in prison. Usually, Major Tremaine did not employ women with such a background. She had proven competent in her work so far, but her delighted greeting for the truculent newcomer did not make the bartender feel any better disposed toward her.

"Hey, Katey, gal!" the cowhand whooped, at the termination of the embrace. "Ain't it a pistol finding you-all here. Barkeep, set up a drink for her and fill it with the real thing, not the cold tea you usually make 'em drink." There was a mocking, challenging sneer on his face as he turned and stepped until he had a clear view of the target on the wall. Glancing at the man behind the bar, he went on, "Just so you-all don't figure you can play li'l ole me for a sucker—"

Leaving the words hanging in the air the blond returned his gaze to the front. Releasing the glass he was holding, he sent his hands to the butts of the Colts. Even as the glass landed on the floor, the Colts were clearing leather to crash almost simultaneously. The speed was such that the bartender considered it to be close to equal to the demonstration given by Doc Leroy the previous evening. Nor, despite firing from almost double the distance, was the youngster addressed by the girl as Waco less accurate than the Wedge cowhand had been. Two holes, less than an inch apart, appeared in the target's left breast.

"Now I'll take me another drink," the youngster announced, twirling away the Colts in a flashy motion and facing the counter, but not offering to pick up the discarded glass. "And fill it right up to the top, hombre."

"Whooee, Waco!" enthused the girl, who went by the

name of Katey Allbright. "You-all haven't changed one li'l bit, nor gotten any slower. Hey, though, is Clay Allison coming here?"

"I wouldn't know, Katey-gal," Waco answered disinterestedly. "Hell, I'm fed to my guts with punching cattle at thirty a month and found. Come on, let's drink 'n' whoop things up a mite."

"I've never been known to say no to *that*," Katey affirmed. "Let's get us a bottle and go sit a spell."

Accepting the suggestion Waco purchased a bottle of whiskey. Collecting two glasses he swept the room with his gaze and, reaching a decision, led the way to a small table not far from the wooden target.

"Howdy," the youngster greeted the two townsmen sitting in front of him. "I'd say's you-all're the kind of gents who wouldn't want to see a lady stand?"

Staring up at Waco, the pair noticed that he held the bottle in his left hand—Katey was carrying the glasses—and the right dangled within easy reach of the Colt it had drawn at such speed a few minutes earlier. While the town's regular deputy sheriff and Jervis Tragg—who was substituting for him during a brief visit to the county seat—were capable of preventing cowhand horseplay from getting out of hand, or halting such abuses, neither was present. Nor were Marshal Arthur Gormley or his deputies in the saloon. So, as they were not fighters, the two men considered discretion to be the better part of valor. Rising, they surrendered their chairs and, as the cowhand and the girl sat down, left the room.

For one with such an arrogant nature and competence in matters *pistolero,* Waco seemed to be displaying a surprising lack of caution. Or it may have been that he was trusting Katey to warn him if danger threatened from behind. In either case he had selected the chair which put his back to the door. However, if he was relying upon her, she failed to justify his confidence. It might have been that she did not recognize the two men who entered while he was pouring out the drinks and was unaware of his connection with them.

They were Dusty Fog and the Ysabel Kid!

The former was half carrying, half dragging a saddle that had a bedroll strapped to its cantle and a Winchester rifle in the boot. Having glanced around, he stalked forward, followed by the Kid, and made for the table at which Waco was sitting. His gait was sharp and suggestive of anger, while his face bore a frown of savage indignation.

Waco's first intimation of the small Texan's arrival came when the saddle landed on the table, knocking the whiskey bottle over.

"What the—?" the youngster began, twisting around and starting to get up as the girl threw over her chair and rose just as hurriedly.

"You idle son of a bitch!" Dusty barked, chopping each word out viciously. "You've left the herd shorthanded after you let two of the boys get bushwhacked this morning. You're fired!"

"So I'll go to work for some other outfit," Waco said with sullen disinterest, but the other customers—who had fallen silent and were watching—saw that he did not offer to reach for a gun.

Only those who failed to identify the small Texan were puzzled by the youngster's passive behavior. The rest, despite having seen his demonstration, did not blame him for refraining when he was faced by the legendary Rio Hondo gun wizard.

"Not around here, you won't!" Dusty warned angrily. "Once I've passed the word about what you've done, nobody will take you on."

"Then I'll easy enough go someplace where they will," Waco answered with uneasy defiance, but his gaze flickered to the saddle—which he identified as his own—on the table.

"Not on any OD Connected horse," Dusty declared flatly. "It's going back to the herd with us!"

"But I don't have a hoss of my own—!" Waco commenced.

"You've only got *yourself* to blame for *that!*" Dusty pointed out.

"You're setting me down?" The youngster almost gasped, being all too aware of what such a thing implied.

"I am," Dusty confirmed, and started to turn away.

"God damn you!" Waco shouted furiously, grabbing the small Texan's right bicep with his left hand and tugging at it. "You'll not set *me* afoot!"

There was not a man, nor hardly a woman, in the barroom who failed to appreciate the youngster's obvious consternation at the prospect of being left without a mount.

To a cowhand in those days of the open ranges, a horse was far more than just a means of transport. It was a vital necessity without which he was unable to carry out the majority of his work or earn a living. Nor could he travel in search of fresh employment should the need arise. Being aware of this a rancher would generally allow a cowhand who was leaving and did not possess a mount of his own to borrow one from the spread's remuda.

However, if the cowhand was dismissed for exceptionally reprehensible behavior, the loan would not be made.

There was no greater disgrace a cowhand could suffer than to be set afoot.*

To have it happen implied that he was worthless and untrustworthy, the kind no other rancher would want to hire. Once the news circulated, he would find it almost impossible to obtain employment in the cattle business.

So, when a cowhand was set afoot, there was certain to be trouble and it might even erupt into gunplay.

On this occasion, however, the latter did not happen.

Waco's anger at the humiliation he was suffering had caused him to act rashly, but he was given no chance to rectify his error.

* The term *set down* had the same connotation as *set afoot.*—J.T.E.

Turning faster than he was being pulled, Dusty threw the grasp from his arm and drove his left fist in a power-packed punch that impacted just below the youngster's breastbone. Then, as Waco began to double over in agony, his other hand whipped up. Its knuckles met the youngster's jaw, lifted him erect, and slammed him backward against the wall.

"You lousy son of a bitch!" Katey screeched, darting around the table with her hands reaching toward Dusty's hair.

Slapping the girl's arms aside before the fingers reached him, the small Texan put the flat of his hand against her face and gave a shove that sent her reeling away to land sitting on the floor. Having done so he caught hold of Waco's shirt-front and prevented the dazed youngster from moving.

"You lousy, no-good son of a bitch!" the small Texan spat furiously, punctuating the words with savage backhand and open-palm blows that snapped Waco's head from side to side.

"Take it easy, amigo," the Kid requested, after several of the blows had been delivered to the helpless and unresisting youngster. "I know he deserves it, but Jervis Tragg wouldn't take kind was you to kill him."

Glancing over his shoulder Dusty nodded. Then he transferred his hands to grasp Waco's calfskin vest. Swinging around he propelled the youngster away from him. Twirling around with no control over his limbs, Waco crashed down to roll over twice. On coming to a halt he made a slight attempt to rise. Then he went limp and subsided to the floor.

"Y-you bastard!" Katey shrieked, glaring at the small Texan as he walked toward the motionless youngster. Rising hurriedly she ran to throw herself in a protective manner across Waco. "Don't you-all dare lay a hand on him again."

"I don't aim to," Dusty replied, reaching into his pants pocket. He pulled out two ten-dollar bills and flung them to the floor, continuing, "Here's all the pay he has coming, and it's more than he deserves. When he starts to take notice, tell him, from me that, if he *ever* comes near Rio Hondo County and I see him, I'll kill him where he stands."

CHAPTER FOURTEEN

THAT'S WHY I SAVED YOUR LIFE

Silkie Roelich realized that he was in considerable peril the moment he saw the two men who were stepping through the door of the apparently deserted house to which he had been directed by Marshal Arthur Gormley. What was more, he felt certain that the municipal peace officer had deliberately sent him into a trap.

Three days had gone by since Deputy Sheriff Jervis Tragg and his posse had paid their eventful visit to the Island Mission. They had not returned, so Roelich was confident that his employer's explanation had been accepted. However, as yet Roelich had been unable to hire any replacements for the quartet of hired guns whose services were lost. With the end of the month and the arrival of the prospective buyers so close, there was a growing need to bring the mission's protective force up to at least its former strength.

So, when a messenger sent by Gormley had arrived with the news that there was a likely prospect available in the town, Roelich had not hesitated to ride in. What the marshal had told him was sufficient for him to consider that the journey might prove to be worthwhile.

Roelich had already heard of how Waco was set afoot by Dusty Fog and, having also been told of the demonstration of gunplay in the Man on the Wall Saloon, wondered if he might be a possible recruit. However, being cautious by nature, he had decided to wait until he knew more about the youngster before making an offer. In addition to telling the marshal to keep an eye on Waco, he had sought information from the other hired guns at the mission. One of them had remembered that the youngster had ridden for Clay Allison and had gained a reputation, even among that wild-onion crew, of being bad medicine. Unfortunately, nobody could say how, or why, Waco had transferred employment to the OD Connected.*

Having so little to go on, Roelich had taken no action with regard to approaching the youngster until he received the marshal's message. According to Gormley the stigma attached to the way that Waco had been discharged from the OD Connected was having an adverse effect. Although he had tried to be hired by three trail bosses, none of them would employ him. Nor, having no horse, was he able to go elsewhere in search of work. To make matters worse, as the news would already be spreading, every day he had to stay in Bannock's Ford further decreased his chances when he finally obtained the means to move on. However, he had twice proved himself to be dangerous. Firstly by repeating his display on the Man on the Wall Saloon's target. Then he had forced two newly arrived Wedge cowhands to back down in a quarrel over a card game.

Satisfied with what he was hearing, Roelich had asked where he might find the youngster. He was told that Waco and a saloon girl were living in the abandoned building from which he, Ivan Petrov, and Gormley had kept watch on the night of Doctor Gollicker's murder. Leaving his horse tied to the hitching rail of the Man on the Wall Saloon, having called there to find that the young cowhand was not present, the boss gun had walked to the house. While it had proved to be occupied, neither of the men who emerged was the one he had come seeking.

Nor were the pair strangers to Roelich!

In their middle thirties, there was a close family likeness about their surly and sneering features. They were tall, well

* Told in TRIGGER FAST.—J.T.E.

built, and dressed after the fashion of successful professional gamblers. Another thing they had in common was that each's right hand hovered not far over the butt of a tied-down Army Colt.

"Howdy, Silkie," greeted Tom, the slightly taller and, as the boss gun—who had come to a halt at the sight of them—was aware, elder of the Scanlon brothers. "It's took us a fair spell to've catched up with you-all."

"That it has," agreed the younger, Jack. "We was right pleased when we got word of where you was hiding out, Silkie-boy."

While they were speaking, the brothers took turns in watching Roelich and darting glances behind him to make sure that he was alone. Even with the odds in their favor and aided by a precaution they had taken, each had too much respect for his prowess to want any unnecessary risks.

"Joey went first," the boss gun pointed out, having no delusions about his danger and chances of survival. Nor did he expect the excuse would be accepted. "What else could I have done?"

"Let him kill you-all," Tom replied. "That'd've saved Jack 'n' me some time 'n' money looking for you to do it."

"It sure would," the younger brother seconded. "So, seeing's you-all gunned poor li'l Joey all nice and legal, Tom 'n' me're allowing to give you the same chance."

"It wouldn't be fair to do anything else," Tom declared.

Suddenly Roelich realized that the brothers were talking far louder than was necessary, or even desirable, under the circumstances. They should have wanted to avoid attracting attention to what would *not* be a fair fight, but murder. Which meant that they must have a smart reason for making so much noise. It could only be for the purpose of drowning out some sound that would convey a warning to their intended victim.

Then Roelich's training and instincts as a *pistolero valiente* supplied the answer. There could be only one reason why the Scanlons had allowed him to come to within about fifteen feet of the house before emerging, instead of making their appearance while he was at a safer distance.

Even as the understanding was creating a sense of alarm, it was verified for the boss gun in no uncertain fashion.

"And us Scanlons're allus fair," Jack stated, throwing a quick look to his right. "So you-all'd best—"

Before the comment could be completed, something happened in the direction to which the younger brother had briefly turned his gaze.

There was a thud such as might be caused by somebody delivering a hard kick to another person, followed immediately by a cry of mingled astonishment and pain. A sawed-off shotgun flew from beyond the corner of the building to land, fortunately—as its hammers were drawn back to fully cocked—without discharging, on the ground. Then a man in untidy range clothes erupted into view. His spine was arched forward in a way that, taken with the agony distorting his unprepossessing features, suggested he had been the recipient of the kick. Blundering forward a few steps he lost his balance and toppled face down after the weapon.

"Get him!" Tom screeched, realizing what the sight implied and commencing his draw.

Just as surprised at the unexpected turn of events, although he had suspected an enemy might be lurking around the corner, Roelich also grabbed for his gun.

So did Jack Scanlon!

Fast though the boss gun knew himself to be, he was just as sure that he could not hope to cope with both of the brothers. While he was shooting one, the other was certain to put lead into him.

Roelich's dilemma was solved by the person who had removed the menace of the Scanlons' concealed ally.

Stepping forward, a pair of Indian moccasins on his feet explaining how he had arrived without his presence being detected by the man he had kicked, Waco turned the scales in the boss gun's favor. He was a factor that the brothers had not anticipated, but Jack responded quickly by trying to deal with him.

Not quickly enough!

Dipping like the strike of an enraged sidewinder,* Waco's right hand brought the Colt from its contoured holster. An educated thumb curled around and drew back the hammer. With just as little need for conscious guidance the forefinger entered the guard and began to squeeze at the trigger only after the barrel was pointing away from him.† Jack's own revolver was still being raised to a point at which it would have proved effective when, aimed at waist level and by instinctive alignment, a .44 caliber bullet was propelled from the muzzle of the blond's weapon. It struck the younger Scanlon in the left breast, knocking him backward and tearing apart his heart, an instant before Roelich sent lead into his brother's head.

Looking around while forcing himself onto hands and knees, the man who should have supported the Scanlons watched them going down. The sight gave him the incentive he needed. Thrusting himself upward, almost like a sprinter taking off at the start of a race, he dashed away as fast as his legs would carry him and without even trying to retrieve the shotgun he had dropped when he was attacked from the rear.

"Looks like he's not all that took with our company," Waco drawled, returning the Colt to its holster.

"Looks that way," Roelich agreed, also replacing his weapon. "How'd you-all come to be on hand?"

"My gal Katey heard the Scanlons, that jasper and that lard-gutted town clown, Gormley, talking over what they aimed to do," the youngster explained. "So I kind of snuck around the back, waited till he come out, and took cards."

* Sidewinder: the subspecies of horned rattlesnake, *Crotalus cerastes,* found mainly in the desert country of the southwestern United States and so called because of its distinctive lateral motions when traveling.—J.T.E.

† An example of how dangerous a failure to carry out this precaution can be is given in THE FAST GUN.—J.T.E.

"I'm right pleased you did," the boss gun declared truthfully. *"Gracias."*

"Hell, I didn't do it for thanks," Waco replied.

"A man doesn't often come across somebody's does what you-all did out of the pure goodness of his heart," Roelich commented interrogatively.

"You still haven't," Waco declared. "I heard tell's you-all're boss gun for some outfit up river a ways and that's why I saved your life. Need me a riding chore, but I've had my fill of punching cattle. So I conclude you owe me a big enough favor to get me taken on."

"I reckon it can be arranged," Roelich said, then looked toward the town's main street. "Here come the folks to find out what all the shooting's been about."

"Don't see no sign of good ole Marshal Gormley, though," Waco answered. "Could be he's been called away urgent like."

"Could be he has," Roelich growled. "Which, next time I come across him, I aim to see he gets called away real permanent. You'd best leave me do the talking—that way there's less chance we'll be held instead of getting let go out to the mission."

"Thishere's Waco, Professor," Silkie Roelich introduced. "I've taken him on as one of the guards."

The boss gun's summation of the situation in Bannock's Ford had proved correct.

One of the earliest arrivals on the scene after the shooting had been Deputy Sheriff Jervis Tragg. Showing no sign of being worried by the blond youngster's reputation as a dangerous and truculent *pistolero,* he had demanded to know what had happened. On hearing Roelich's story he had conceded that the killings were done in self-defense. However, when he questioned Waco—who surprised Roelich by answering without any display of arrogance—he had discovered that an old score had been settled. The Scanlon brothers had once cheated and killed one of the youngster's friends. Realizing that he could not hope to press charges against either man, Tragg had stated pointedly that Waco's presence in the town was no longer considered desirable. Once again the youngster had displayed remarkable restraint. He had merely answered that, having been hired by Roelich, he would leave as soon as he had collected his gear and hired a horse.

Dismissed by the deputy the boss gun had accompanied Waco to the room he was sharing with the saloon girl in a small and cheap rooming house. She was still in bed when they arrived and clearly had had no doubts about the outcome of the incident. Nor did she raise any objections when the youngster informed her that he was leaving. Promising that he would drop by and see her as often as possible, he had picked up his belongings and gone to obtain a horse from the livery barn.

During the ride to the Island Mission, Roelich had learned that Waco changed from Clay Allison's CA to the OD Connected in the mistaken belief that it would be a softer outfit to work for. He had soon become disillusioned. Reading between the lines regarding the reason for his having been fired and set afoot, the boss gun decided that he had been sleeping instead of riding night herd when Mexican bandidos raided the trail drive's camp. Then, taking advantage of Mark Counter's absence, he had run out only to fall foul of Dusty Fog, who he had not known was in the vicinity.

On reaching the mission's houses by the bank of the river, Roelich had told Waco to settle in and had crossed to the Island. He soon returned with his employer, to whom he had obviously reported what had happened in Bannock's Ford. They had come back together and the youngster was summoned to the boss gun's private quarters.

"Waco?" Professor Hogreth Morbeus said. "Is that all?"

"Knowed a feller one time who'd got five real fancy names to his handle," the youngster replied, deciding that his employer—who was wearing a check suit and florid silk cravat —looked more like a jovial bartender than a man of medicine. "But they sure's hell didn't help him much when he tried to pull a gun on *me*."

"What happened to him?" Morbeus inquired.

"He died of a case of slow," Waco explained with a hard grin.

"I thought he might have," Morbeus admitted, knowing what the term implied. "And I hope that you enjoy working here."

"I don't like *working* anyplace," the youngster corrected frankly. "But, just so the pay's good and I'm not having to ride herd on a bunch of stinking cattle, I reckon I'll get by."

"What do you think?" Roelich asked, after Waco had been dismissed and left the room.

"He *seems* to be all right," Morbeus replied, for the boss gun had mentioned certain misgivings while they were crossing from the island. "But, as you said, he was working for the OD Connected and Fog didn't strike me as the kind of man who would make many mistakes when it came to hiring hands. On the other hand I agree that if he found out he had, or one he'd taken on let him down that badly, he'd probably react like he did. And, once *he'd* set somebody afoot, most other cattlemen would fight shy of hiring him."

"That's for sure, from what the kid told me," Roelich conceded. "But it still seems to me there're a whole slew of coincidences mixed in it."

"There are," Morbeus admitted, frowning pensively. "But he saved your life and had to kill a man to do it, which is a big step to take if he should be up to something."

"It is," the boss gun concurred. "Only, even if he hadn't had an old score to settle with the Scanlons, once he cut in Jack didn't give him any choice but to throw lead. Then there's that gal of his. I've got the feeling's I've seen her afore, but I can't bring to mind where or when."

"It must have been in some saloon or other—her kind move around a lot," Morbeus pointed out, then recalled another matter and went on, "By the way, did you see anything of that woman author while you were in town this time?"

"Nope," Roelich answered. "And I never thought to ask about her, comes to that. Which, after the way he set me up for the Scanlons, I don't reckon's that bastard Gormley's going to be around to tell me anything next time I go in. I'll bet he's long gone and's looking for a hole so's he can hide from me—" Struck by a thought that had arisen from that aspect, he paused for a moment and then continued, "Hey, though! Will that game Petrov pulled on him keep working after he's run out?"

"It will, so far as I know," Morbeus replied, having had certain precautions taken against a betrayal of their activities. "But we'd better ask and make sure. I want him over here, anyway. Providing that youngster is all right, we can use somebody as good as he is with a gun. If he's not, he's been planted on us because Fog and Tragg didn't believe what I told them about the anthrax and are trying to find out the truth."

"I'll pass the word for Petrov to come on over," Roelich promised, standing up. "He'll settle which it is for us easy enough."

CHAPTER FIFTEEN

I DON'T AIM TO TAKE CHANCES

"The influence I have put upon Gormley will continue to work, no matter where he is, until I take it off again," Ivan Petrov declared, his heavily accented voice displaying complete confidence. He was sitting in Silkie Roelich's lamplit quarters shortly after sundown and was answering the point that had been raised earlier by the boss gun. "Other subjects I have 'mesmerized'—as *you* will call it—in the same manner have continued to respond to my instructions for many months. As he has already suffered the head pains that I have conditioned him to feel if he should try to speak of what we are doing to anyone other than the three of us, he will have no wish to experience them again. Or they will strike him with just as much severity as it did Hooper if he should try to betray us in the future."

"So you're satisfied he won't talk, Ivan?" Professor Hogreth Morbeus asked.

"I am," Petrov confirmed with absolute assurance. "There is nothing to fear from him, my friend."

"I'd still sooner the son of a bitch was dead, but that's just personal," Roelich growled, having seen enough to make him willing to accept the swarthy Mid-European's summation. "How about that kid Waco?"

"Bring him in," Petrov replied. "Once he's under my influence, he will tell you *everything* you want to know."

The Mid-European's ability as a hypnotist—although the

word had not yet come into general usage*—had made him a vital factor in Morbeus's schemes. It had been Petrov who provided the means by which the secret process for turning a human being into a "zombie" had been extracted from a voodoo priest in Haiti. He had also helped to collect and control the specimens concealed in the Island Mission. In addition he ensured that no word of their presence leaked out. The latter had been achieved by inducing a state of posthypnotic suggestion upon the few of Morbeus's employees, two of whom were Town Marshal Arthur Gormley and the late Toby Hooper, who knew what was happening inside the building. Once under the influence each would experience the most violent headache if he attempted to mention the zombies to anybody other than Petrov, Morbeus, or Roelich. The professor and the boss gun had already seen how effectively it worked when Hooper had started to become indiscreet.

"This is my assistant, Mr. Petrov," Morbeus introduced, when the blond youngster had arrived and had been seated opposite the Mid-European at the table. "I suppose you're wondering what we're doing out there on the island?"

"Not specially," Waco drawled laconically. "Just so long's I get told what you want me to do and pay me, that's all I need to keep me happy."

"It's something you'll have to know, though," Morbeus stated, in an amiable tone. "But first of all I'd like to carry out a little test."

"What kind of test?" Waco demanded suspiciously.

"Nothing hard, or dangerous," Morbeus replied reassuringly, interlocking his fingers and laying his hands on the top of the table. "This is all you have to do."

* Until the English physician James Braid made a detailed study of the subject in the middle of the nineteenth century and coined the expression *hypnosis*—from the Greek word *hypnōtikos*—sleep-hypnotism was generally referred to as "mesmerism" in honor of the Viennese practitioner Franz A. Mesmer (1733–1815), whose use of it had attracted considerable attention—and, due to its being inadequately understood, it received not a little criticism—during the latter part of the previous century.—J.T.E.

"Looks easy enough," Waco admitted and duplicated the action.

"Look into my eyes!" Petrov said, almost caressingly, staring with fixed intensity at the youngster's face when he was obeyed. At the same time he lifted the small crystal globe from where he had kept it hidden beneath the table and, by swirling the chain, caused it to revolve and scintillate brilliantly in the lamplight. "Look deep into my eyes! Clasp your hands tighter! Tighter yet! Even tighter! Now they are growing together! You cannot open—"

At which point the Mid-European discovered that his proposed victim was not succumbing to an old established method of testing a subject's susceptibility to hypnosis.

Coming away from its mate with no difficulty Waco's right hand dipped and rose swiftly. The muzzle of the Army Colt it had drawn during the brief disappearance from view was lined at Petrov's head and the hammer clicked back to fully cocked.

"Saw a jasper in a medicine show pull a game like that one time," the youngster remarked, in a mocking and faintly threatening tone. "Feller he did it to started to do all fool kind of things when he said so. Which I don't cotton to the notion of being made to do something foolish."

"Take it easy, young man," Morbeus said quietly but urgently. "No offence. It was only a joke."

"So was the game those jaspers up to Dodge played with the drummer and the monkey," Waco replied coldly, lowering the Colt's hammer as Petrov returned the globe to his pocket. "Trouble was, the *monkey* got killed."*

"Once you-all find out what we're doing, you'll see why we have to be careful," Roelich commented, having heard of the incident to which the youngster was referring.

* The event to which Waco referred was recorded in the "The Joke" episode of the first—Brown Watson, Ltd., Wagon Wheel Western—edition of THE FASTEST GUN IN TEXAS, *but* omitted in subsequent editions as it did not fit into the time period of the other episodes. A revised version will be included in J. T.'s HUNDREDTH.—J.T.E.

"You-all figure's I *have* to know, go ahead and tell me," Waco countered, his whole bearing redolent of absolute disinterest. "But, like I said, just so long's it don't take in doing any heavy lifting, riding the blister end of a shovel, or working cattle, I don't give two whoops and a holler 'bout what I'm here to do so long's the wages come in large and regular."

"I think we can promise you that you won't have to do any of them and you'll be paid regularly enough," Morbeus answered, oozing what might have been joviality. "Well, gentlemen, I don't think we need waste any more of our young friend here's time."

"One thing, though," Roelich put in, as Waco shoved back his chair and started to stand up. "From today until the end of next week at least we're going to need you-all here *all* the time. There's no way we could spare you to go into town."

"Now, *there's* a relief," the youngster replied with a grin. "That Katey's sure a hell of a dee-manding woman and takes a whole heap of keeping happy in bed, regular's she wants it. I'm near enough so obliged to be given reason to stay clear of her, I'd work for less money—only *near enough,* mind, not all the way there."

"Then we'll not ask you to take less," Morbeus chortled, still exuding bonhomie. "I'm all for a young feller who knows the value of money. You've brought us a good *man* here, Mr. Roelich." However, after Waco had left the room, his mood changed to somber and he asked, "Well, how about him now?"

"He's nobody's fool, that's for sure," Roelich estimated grimly. "And I'd not want to lock horns with him head to head in a poker game. Which I still don't know a whole heap more than I did when he came in."

"I don't trust him!" Petrov stated aggrievedly. "He knew that I was trying to hypnotize him!"

"That don't prove sic 'em one way or t'other, 'cepting he keeps his eyes open," Roelich objected. "I've seen what you-all did pulled in medicine shows as well. All I *know* is he's either genuine, or a right cagy playacting son of a bitch. But don't go asking me which it is."

"Then what do *you* suggest?" Morbeus inquired, having developed considerable faith in his boss gun's judgment.

"If he's all right, we've got a good man on our side," Roelich replied. "But if he's not, I want to keep him around until it's safe to kill him. Put him with the guard on the island, even though he hasn't been fixed to get the headaches like the rest of 'em. Then you can leave one of the gates in the wall open, and if he goes into the mission, we'll know he's a whole heap more interested than he lets on."

"Look out, there!" Waco said urgently, pointing toward the Mexican bank of the Rio Grande.

"What is it?" demanded the hired gun to whom the words had been directed, turning his attention from the small stern-wheeler steamboat that was just entering from the downstream end of the river's Mission Lake region. "I don't see nothing!"

"How about stars?" the youngster inquired, deftly raising and propelling the butt of his Winchester Model of 1866 rifle beneath the brim of the man's hat and against the back of the skull it was otherwise protecting.

Even before the third word was completed, the man was collapsing unconscious. Throwing a glance across the water to find out whether the guards in Mexico had seen what he had done, Waco then assured himself that the high wall surrounding the mission's main buildings had also prevented the two hired guns keeping watch over the boats and landing stage from becoming aware of his activities. With the precautions against discovery taken he had laid down his rifle. Using his victim's waist belt, bandana, and large pocket handkerchief as bonds and a gag, he made sure that he would not be interrupted from that source. With the task completed he hauled the secured man farther into the shadows beyond the light thrown by the fires in the cressets.

Silkie Roelich's misgivings had been justified!

In spite of all that had been said about Waco and the way he had behaved after his return to Bannock's Ford, he was a loyal and dependable—if recent—member of the OD Connected's floating outfit.* Far from having been responsible for what had happened to the trail drive, it had been due mainly to his courage that the raiders did not achieve a greater success.

Demonstrating his ability to make use of any opportunity that was presented, which had been a major factor in his successes as a cavalry raider during the War between the States, Dusty Fog had seen how it might be possible to turn the bandidos' attack to his advantage. The way in which the messenger had acted suggested that the result was not too serious. So, on hearing Waco's name mentioned, the small Texan had gambled upon the old cowhand supplying the required response to his furious "accusation."

Having established the blond youngster as the "culprit," Dusty had given private instructions to Mark Counter. Then, consulting with Belle Boyd and Deputy Sheriff Jervis Tragg, he had formulated the rest of the scheme. Removing her red wig to expose her short hair—which had been dyed blond for her previous assignment and had not yet returned to its natural black—and changing into appropriate attire from her trunks, the girl had become "Katey Allbright" instead of "Elvira Porterham." If anybody had inquired after the latter, they would have been told that she had left to rejoin her husband. The owner of the Man on the Wall Saloon had served in the same regiment as Dusty and had been willing to help the scheme by "hiring" Belle in her new identity.

From the beginning everything had gone smoothly. The arrival of the rest of the Wedge trail crew had produced help to strengthen the belief that Waco was a none-too-honest young hardcase who was willing to take chances for money. An added and unexpected bonus had been Gormley having informed the Scanlon brothers of Roelich's whereabouts

* Details of Waco's background and special qualifications are to be found in APPENDIX FOUR.—J.T.E.

and Belle overhearing his conversation with them. Although Waco's story of having a grudge to settle had been untrue, he was aware of their far from savory reputation and had known each to be a ruthless killer. So he had had neither moral scruples over his intervention, nor remorse because of the result.

While they had been "living" together, Belle had among other things warned Waco of Petrov's ability as a hypnotist. She had also suggested how the Mid-European's talent might be implemented, which had prepared the youngster for the danger when it had come. Helped by Jervis Tragg's knowledge of local affairs, she and Dusty—who had returned to the town secretly after supposedly having joined the raided trail herd in Mexico—had formulated a plan of campaign.

Much to the deputy's surprise Belle had taken the small Texan's comments about voodoo and zombies seriously when they were discussing the reason for the government of Haiti's interest in Morbeus. Born and raised on a plantation in Louisiana, she knew enough about Negroes not to discount all hex-throwers and conjure-women as mere charlatans, being aware that some of them were capable of producing extraordinary—even inexplicable—effects. However, she had felt that the creation of a zombie resulted from the administration of some form of narcotic compound developed over the years by the voodoo priests and did not arise from any supernatural powers.

When Tragg had asked to what use such knowledge could be put, Belle had pointed out that the authorities in Haiti were alleged to employ voodoo as a means of enforcing their will on the population. France, Spain, and Portugal all had colonies in Africa, with large numbers of simple natives who believed in witchcraft, magic, and the supernatural to be kept under control. There were also many primitive peons and Indians in Mexico who might find such powers an inducement to good behavior.* So, as she was unable to

* The documents in the possession of the Hardin, Fog, and Blaze clan that were made available to the author suggest that Miss Boyd's theories were

171

think of anything else to which the government of Haiti might attach such importance, she was willing to keep an open mind on the matter.

Three days had elapsed since Waco's meeting with Roelich. In spite of having been given a thorough education in the basic elements of conventional law enforcement since throwing in his lot with Dusty,* the youngster had had neither training for nor experience in the kind of task he was performing. For all that, his intelligence and the guidance he had received from the Rebel Spy—an authority on such deceptions—had carried him through. He was also helped by having been until recently much the sort of person he was portraying. So, although he had sensed that Morbeus, Roelich, and Petrov were not entirely convinced he was what he pretended to be, he had avoided confirming their suspicions.

Since entering Morbeus's employment Waco had had no opportunity to pass on what little information he had gathered. Nor was he intended to do so, other arrangements having been made. These had further demonstrated Dusty's ability to deduce what line of action the opposition might take. His estimation of what would possibly happen to the youngster had proved correct.

Being suspicious, as the small Texan had anticipated might happen, Morbeus and Roelich had offered Waco the means by which he could have exposed his true purpose. He had never been sent out with the wood-gathering parties that were dispatched each day. Instead, he was kept at the buildings on the riverbank and, every night, he had been included in the four-man guard who patrolled the island to keep the cressets supplied with fuel and the steam launch's

---

valid. However, there was no explanation of the means employed to create the "zombies." Alvin Dustine "Cap" Fog—some details of whose career are given in "Cap" Fog, Texas Ranger, Meet Mr. J. G. Reeder—told us that his grandfather and Miss Boyd had considered the information was too dangerous to commit to paper in case it should fall into the wrong hands. Considering the state of the world today, we are in complete agreement.—J.T.E.

* How is told in The Making of a Lawman and The Trouble Busters.—J.T.E.

boiler stoked up ready for an immediate departure. Although the professor and Petrov had spent the hours of darkness at the mission no matter what the boss gun was doing, none of the quartet had been allowed inside the walls, and all of the gates were kept closed.

Exhibiting what may have been a hereditary flair for such work,* Waco had steered clear of the traps that were set for him. He had resisted the temptation to try to enter the mission's compound, nor had he even tested his belief that a gate had been left unfastened so that he might betray himself. By showing no particular desire to find out what was being done on the island, he had elicited such little information as the hired guns had to offer. He now knew that, in addition to the guard on the island, the protective force was divided into two groups. One stayed in the buildings on the Texas bank and the other kept watch from an adobe line shack at the opposite side of the river.

Although the youngster had learned a few details of the security arrangements, he was unable to find out why only seven of the men alternated as the island's guard. All he knew was that whoever went on duty had to blacken his face with burnt cork before crossing from the living quarters. When he had queried the matter with Roelich, he was told it was to persuade anybody who passed after dark that they were Negro workers and not armed guards. Despite Waco having been assigned to the duty, the seven had been reticent about what it entailed. They had told him only what was expected of him and, if any of them were aware that the murderer of Doctor Gollicker had escaped, it was never mentioned.

Waco might have been prevented from communicating directly with his companions, but he was not completely cut off from them. Traces of Belle's original reconnaissances had been discovered, but it would have taken better men

---

* Neither the author nor fictionist genealogist Philip José Farmer, with whom he consulted, have been able to trace Waco's family background beyond his adoption by the Texas rancher Sunshine Sam Catlan.—J.T.E.

than any of the hired guns to locate signs that the Ysabel Kid was keeping them under observation.

At the appointed time the previous evening Waco had seen three brief flickers of light on the downstream fringe of the woodland. They had notified him that, providing he could do his part, the plans that had been made in Bannock's Ford were to be put into effect the following night. Asking Roelich if he could go and visit "Katey" the next afternoon, he was told it would not be possible as he was required for guard duty on the island. Having acquired the vital information, he had contrived to make the prearranged signal to that effect.

The day had been as leisurely and uneventful as its predecessors for Waco. There was nothing to be seen or heard that could have served as a warning of the various preparations being carried out by his friends. At sundown, having applied the obligatory burnt cork to his face and hands, he had accompanied three of the hired guns to the island. They retained one of the rowboats after delivering five men to the line cabin in Mexico. The other was left tied to the landing stage on the Texas bank and any communication from the island would be carried across in the canoe.

At last, having heard the whoop of the *Ranchero II*'s whistle from downstream, the youngster had known the time for action was drawing near. As both of the owners were Dusty's friends, he had been confident that whoever was in command would be cooperative, and the sound confirmed his belief was justified. So Waco had set about his task.

Despite having disposed of the first guard without difficulty, the youngster knew there was no time to spare. The *Ranchero II* was not moving at full speed, but it was still approaching quickly enough for any delay to endanger the rest of the plan. As he retrieved his rifle and started to walk around the end of the perimeter wall, he kept his ears working to detect any suggestion that the party in Mexico had noticed what was being towed by the steamboat. If all was going well, however, their attention should be held by members of the Wedge crew who were beyond the skyline and endeavoring to make them think bandidos were lurking there contemplating mischief.

Reaching the front end of the wall, without having heard any alarm raised from south of the river, Waco did not care for what he discovered when he looked around the corner. He had hoped to find both of the remaining hired guns together, but only one was in sight. Standing in the steam launch and tossing a few logs on to the boiler's fire, he would present no great problem. It was his missing companion who could create the difficulty. However, the one in the boat must be dealt with as quickly as possible.

As he advanced toward the landing stage, the youngster gazed about him in the hope of locating the last of the immediate obstacles to his friends' safe arrival on the island. Morbeus and Petrov were at the mission, but had never come outside during his previous nights on duty. So there were only the two gunhands to be disposed of to make the invasion successful.

"Hey, Sudsy," Waco called, strolling in an almost casual seeming manner along the landing stage. "Where at's Boker?"

"Went round to see if either of you'all'd got the makings," the man replied, and glanced across the water. "Wonder if that boat's fetched in any of them fellers the boss's expecting?"

"I dunno," Waco grunted, knowing that—although the main channel passed between the island and Mexico—it was possible for the shallow-draft steamboats to reach and unload at the landing stage. "Will it be coming in here?"

"Don't look like it's aiming to," the man decided, starting to climb from the launch. "We'd've been told if it—"

"Sudsy! Dray! Waco!" yelled the voice of the missing guard from beyond the building. "Get back here, pronto!"

Bounding into range Waco swung up his Winchester. Caught under the jaw while still in the process of coming onto the landing stage, Sudsy was pitched backward. Even as he fell into the launch, with his head striking the side and rendering him unconscious, his assailant spun around and went racing toward the speaker.

Cowhand boots were not the most suitable footwear for running, but Waco set the best pace he could manage. On passing alongside the wall he saw the last of the hired guns some distance away. The man was pointing a rifle toward the rowing boat that, having been towed upriver by the *Ranchero II,* had cast off and was approaching the island as fast as its oars could propel it.

"Drop it, Boker!" the youngster shouted, skidding to a halt with the butt of the Winchester rising toward his shoulder and silently cursing what he knew was almost certain to come next.

"Wha—?" the hired gun began, glancing over his shoulder.

Instantly a realization of what Waco had said and was doing struck Boker. Self-preservation rather than loyalty to his employer motivated his reaction. Spitting out a furious obscenity he swiveled his weapon in the youngster's direction.

The two rifles went off at almost the same instant!

Feeling the Stetson being torn from his head, until its flight was restrained by the *barbiquejo,* Waco saw the hired gun's body jerk as his bullet struck home. Working the lever to reload and ready to shoot again, he resumed his advance. He saw that he would not need the weapon. Throwing aside the rifle as the lead had torn through his chest and spun him in a circle, Boker went down.

"Damn it to hell!" Waco spat out, hearing faint shouts of alarm from the buildings on either side of the river and knowing that the shots would have been even more audible to the occupants of the mission.

"Good work, boy," Dusty praised, shortly after the youngster's sotto voce comment, although he had hoped the landing would be carried out in silence. Leaping over the bows as the boat ran aground while still some feet from the island, an example followed by its other passengers, he waded rapidly ashore and continued, "You and Lon make sure none of the bunch on the north bank try to come over before the posse gets down from the woods. You and Tarbrush do the same on this side, Doc."

"Sure," grinned the Kid, looking at the Wedge cowhand. "Then, when them yahoos from Mexico get here 'n' kill us, it'll be *your* no-account outfit's to blame." At that moment he noticed Waco's face. Previously he had not been close enough to discover the precaution that the men guarding the island had been compelled to carry out. "Hey, you-all look better that way, boy."

"*You* couldn't look good *any* way," the youngster countered, delighted to have found that Dusty—whose opinion and friendship he admired more than that of any other person—was not angry over his failure to quell all the guards without gunplay.

"Let's go!" Dusty ordered, holding two fused sticks of dynamite in his left hand and a hooded lantern in the right. "If there's any delay, shout and let us know so that we can wait and all try to go in at the same time."

Knowing what was expected of them and equipped in the same general manner as the small Texan, Belle Boyd—who was bareheaded, clad in a man's black shirt, riding breeches, Hessian boots, and armed with an ivory handled Dance Bros. Navy revolver, butt forward in the contoured holster tied to her right thigh—Mark Counter and Jervis Tragg separated to attend to the tasks that had been assigned to them.

CHAPTER SIXTEEN

LEAVE THEM TO THE *ZOMBIES*

"Well, Ivan, the first of our customers should be in Bannock's Ford soon," Professor Hogreth Morbeus remarked, gazing complacently around the laboratory he had had set up in the largest ground-floor room of the Island Mission's main building. "Let's hope they don't recognize each other if they all come up from Brownsville on the *Ranchero II*. Or if they do, that none tries to stop the others reaching us."

"Would they do that?" Ivan Petrov inquired.

"I don't see any reason why they should," Morbeus replied. "When I contacted them, I didn't hide the fact that we're offering the technique to the other countries and at the same price." He frowned for a moment, then asked, "Are you sure there won't be any trouble with the other zombie we brought from Haiti?"

"It's not acting like the one that broke out," the Mid-European answered sullenly, making no attempt to hide his resentment at being reminded how an error on his part had allowed the big Negro to escape and endangered their project. "There's nothing to worry about. If we have any doubts, we can hide it and show the ones we've created since we came here."

"It might be better if we do that anyway," Morbeus stated. "They might not look as hideous, but they'll do everything it will. With the kind of money that's at stake, we don't want anything to go wrong."

Even before he had qualified as a surgeon, the professor

—a title he had conferred upon himself—had been fascinated by the subject of longevity. Assisted by two other members of General Smethurst's medical staff during the War between the States who shared his interest,* he had taken advantage of his official position to carry out experiments on Confederate prisoners of war. As this had been done with the knowledge and approval of their superior officer and his political faction, the trio had been allowed to evade the consequences when rumors concerning their activities had caused an investigation by the Union army's adjutant general. Fearing that they would be marked for southron vengeance, despite the way in which the war was going, he had separated from his associates and adopted the name Morbeus.

Still intrigued by the possibility of extending the length of life and being wealthy, the professor had decided to try to find out if zombies offered an answer. Meeting with and learning of Petrov's prowess as a hypnotist, Morbeus had secured his services and they had visited Haiti. While there, they had not only discovered how to transform a human being into a "zombie," but contrived to smuggle two Negroes who had been subjected to the treatment back to the United States.

With Petrov to keep the original pair of zombies under control, and to help transform three Negroes they had kidnapped since their return, Morbeus had found a safe haven from which to carry out their schemes. Purchasing the Island Mission he had blackmailed a few now prominent politicians who had belonged to the late General Smethurst's clique into presenting him with letters of introduction. They had also produced the names of men serving in various countries' diplomatic corps who might be interested in learning a means by which large populations of illiterate,

* What happened to Professor Morbeus's two associates is told in HELL IN THE PALO DURO and GO BACK TO HELL.—J.T.E.

backward, and superstitious people could be kept subservient.*

At first there had been few snags. Then one of the Haitian zombies had started to misbehave and they had coupled the shackle bands already on its wrists together with a length of chain, which it had subsequently snapped in a paroxysm of strength. Petrov's overconfidence and negligence had allowed it to escape from the mission. However, despite the concern its departure had caused, the affair had passed over. In fact, Morbeus was beginning to believe that Silkie Roelich's misgivings over the young cowhand Waco were groundless. He was also taking comfort from the thought that the representatives of the various countries would soon come and, with the sales made, he would be able to leave Texas forever.

"Nothing can go wrong with them," Petrov promised, and his swarthy face came as close as it ever managed to smiling. "Nor with the sale, as we have nothing written down until we've been paid. So—!"

"What the hell?" Morbeus barked, as the hypnotist's words were brought to an end by the sound of two rifle shots very close together from somewhere at the rear of the building. "Come on!"

Dashing from the laboratory the two men went just as rapidly up the stairs to the first floor. There, they hurried to a window that would allow them to investigate. Although the surrounding wall restricted their view, they could see a strange rowing boat grounded in the shallows. At the edge of the island a Texas cowhand and a Negro in similar attire, each holding a rifle, stood gazing toward the Mexican bank of the river. Not far from them Boker lay sprawled motionless on the ground.

"God damn!" Petrov shouted in his native language, then

---

* At the risk of appearing chauvinistic, the author is pleased to be able to record that, according to the documents he has seen, the British government of the day refused to even consider Professor Morbeus's offer.—J.T.E.

made an effort and returned to English. "Somebody has landed. Are they from one of the buyers?"

"No, those two were with Fog!" Morbeus corrected angrily. "So that tricky son of a bitch wasn't fooled after all. He must have sent that young bastard here!"

"What are we going to do?" Petrov wanted to know.

"That boat can't have brought many of them here," Morbeus estimated. "So we'll stay in here until—"

However, before the professor could complete his suggestion that they wait for the hired guns to arrive and save them, gunfire from both sides of the river warned that help might be delayed or not even be forthcoming.

"They'll be breaking in here soon!" Petrov almost screeched.

"Go and collect your property and we'll leave them to the zombies!" Morbeus replied, having insisted that they be prepared for such an eventuality. "While that's happening, we'll go over the wall and get away in the steam launch."

As the professor was running to his bedroom, he was thankful for the foresight he had shown in keeping only sufficient money for his immediate needs at the mission. He had deposits in banks at Bannock's Ford and Brownsville as well as his main account in New Orleans. So he would not lack funds for the flight that was almost certainly to be necessary.

Collecting his jacket, with all his ready cash in its pockets, a revolver, and a loaded double-barreled shotgun, Morbeus went to a window on the eastern side of the building. Opening it while waiting for Petrov, who arrived armed in the same way, he climbed through on the flat roof of a shelter that extended to the perimeter wall. Leading the way across he was just throwing over a rope attached to a hook on the wall when there was an explosion and the gate to his right was blown open. Similar sounds occurred almost simultaneously from the other three sides, warning that entrances were being effected there by the same means.

"I'll go first," the professor growled, passing his weapon to the hypnotist, and grasping the rope with both hands, he lowered himself over the wall. "Drop the guns to me when I get down. Then we'll run for the boat and kill anybody who tries to stop us."

Having uncovered her lantern so that she could not only see what she was doing, but had the means to light the fuse of the dynamite she was carrying, Belle Boyd placed the stick under the single gate in the mission's eastern wall. Then she waited for either Dusty Fog's signal, or one of the others to announce that he was not yet ready.

A few seconds ticked by, punctuated by a commotion on both of the Rio Grande's banks as the posse from Bannock's Ford and the Wedge cowhands charged toward the buildings with the intention of preventing reinforcements leaving for the island.

"Let her blow!" the small Texan's voice thundered, as he realized that there was no longer any point in trying to conceal their presence by giving the call of a whippoorwill.

Hearing the words and duplicating the speaker's actions the Rebel Spy, Mark Counter at the rear double gates, and Deputy Sheriff Jervis Tragg by the single entrance in the western side each applied a light to the fuse in their explosive charges and withdrew to a safe distance.

When the dynamite he had placed went off, Dusty saw the massive front gates burst asunder. Leaving the lantern on the ground he advanced and became aware of an enormous figure that was lumbering rapidly across the courtyard toward him. It was a Negro with an equally hideous set of features, deliberately worsened by the voodoo priest controller to enhance his awesome appearance, to those of the man who had attacked him on the banks of the small stream.

At the rear Mark's detonation had produced a less successful result. Instead of blasting the way clear it had only caused the two portions of the gate to open a few inches. Returning the Colts to their holsters he ran forward. Aware that time was of great importance he ducked his left shoulder and charged the near side section. It yielded more easily than he had expected. Stumbling through he found himself confronted by a charging, half-naked colored man who almost matched his height, weighed heavier, and bulged with what were obviously immensely powerful muscles.

Although Belle effected her entrance without difficulty, her problems commenced as she went through the ruined gateway. Being on the side of the establishment that was in the shadows, she carried the Dance in her right hand ready for instant use and had retained the lantern in the other. Hearing footsteps to her left she glanced in that direction. What she discovered was highly disconcerting. On seeing her, instead of following Professor Morbeus over the wall, Ivan Petrov dropped one of the shotguns he was holding. She did not need to wonder why he had done so. Nor did she believe that he was intending to use the other weapon to defend her against the massive zombie who was emerging from the shelter upon the roof of which he was standing.

Like the Rebel Spy, Jervis Tragg was carrying a cocked gun—but had left his lantern behind—as he arrived in the compound. Seeing the gigantic, glaring-eyed Negro who was approaching in a threatening fashion, he doubted whether he would get anywhere with verbal reasoning. Nor would he have a chance at close quarters against such a heavier and muscular assailant. However, as he was far from a cold-blooded killer, he lined his Colt and sent a bullet into the man's shoulder. For all the result he achieved, he might have thrown a spitball. Nearer rushed the Negro. The deputy fired again, this time into the broad black chest—but the man still came on without showing any effect from what should have been an incapacitating wound.

Completing the descent of the rope Morbeus looked up. There was no sign of the hypnotist, so he opened his mouth to bellow a command for haste in dropping the shotgun.

As Tragg had, Dusty appreciated that there was no hope of stopping his attacker without gunplay. However, his last experience with a zombie suggested how to deal with the situation. Crossing with extreme rapidity, his hands swept the matched Army Colts from their holsters. Turning outward as if of their own volition, so perfectly did he coordinate the movements, they roared at the same instant, slightly over three quarters of a second after he had commenced his draw. Each bullet went into the zombie's head, shattering the brain and toppling him lifeless to the ground.

With an effort Mark retained his balance. Instead of trying to halt and take action he kept going. Bounding into the air he sent his right foot crashing on to the center of the huge Negro's chest. Immune to pain though the treatment to which he had been subjected made him, not even the man's great bulk could fend off such an attack. He was thrown backward several feet by the impulsion of the blond giant's two-hundred-and-eighteen-pound body. While he did not go down, by the time he had come to a stop, Mark was alighting from delivering the kick. Watching the man returning, the big blond drew the right hand Colt and, profiting from the small Texan's advice, shot him between the eyes as the only way of stopping him.

Displaying the fluid speed which made her so capable as a savate fighter, Belle launched herself into a graceful yet deadly pirouette. She employed some of the impetus gathered in the turn to propel the lantern at the Negro's head. Making the desired contact it shattered and its fuel ignited to engulf the black face in flames. Aghast at the sight she forced herself to continue thinking and acting. A leap carried her clear of the burning zombie and he blundered onward.

Landing, Belle saw that Petrov was raising the shotgun. With her left hand joining and supporting the right, she elevated the Dance even more quickly. Displaying the kind of accuracy that had saved Tarbrush from Toby Hooper, she planted a .36 caliber ball in the center of the hypnotist's chest. He took an involuntary step to the rear, striking the wall and tumbling over with the weapon leaving his grasp as he disappeared.

Having been sent by Doc Leroy to help, when it was obvious that the guards on the Mexican bank were fully occupied, Tarbrush came into the compound through the east gate as the Rebel Spy shot Petrov. He used the bullet from his Ballard to end whatever suffering the flame-encrusted zombie might have been experiencing.

Until the failure of his second shot to elicit any response from its recipient, Tragg had not been convinced that such things as zombies could exist. However, faced with a human being who could withstand two bullets and still keep coming, he found that his point of view was undergoing a drastic revision. Retreating a couple of strides and thumb-cocking the Colt, he sent the third load to where he hoped it would achieve its purpose. As a hole appeared just above the Negro's staring eyes, he seemed to crumple. Buckling in midstride his legs deposited him face down at the deputy's feet.

Before Morbeus could speak, he saw Petrov take Belle's lead. Jumping aside as the hypnotist toppled from above, the professor managed to catch the discarded shotgun. He manipulated it into a firing position while running to the front end of the wall. As he had feared, he found on passing beyond the corner that there were sufficient invaders for a guard to be placed over the steam launch. However, as they had apparently decided that their presence was not needed and no reinforcements would be coming from the buildings on the Texas bank, they were making their way toward the front gate.

Until Morbeus noticed one of the pair was Waco, he had contemplated surrendering and trusting his political associates—under the threat of his betrayal of their secrets—to save him from the ultimate penalty for his misdeeds. Savage fury gripped him at the sight of the youngster who, despite a lack of formal education, had tricked him and been a major factor in his downfall. Snarling with anger he started to elevate the butt of the shotgun toward his shoulder.

It proved to be the "professor's" final mistake!

Lacking the time to aim in a formal fashion the Kid and Waco pivoted their Winchesters no higher than waist level. Firing fast and moving the barrels in a horizontal arc while operating the levers, they directed their shots like spokes extending from the center of a wheel. Encompassed in the torrent of flying lead Morbeus was swept off his feet without having a chance to return the fire. When his body was examined, there were four bullets in it—any one of which would have proved fatal—as evidence of the pair's unorthodox effectiveness.

"Well, it's over and I'm not sorry we haven't found anything to tell us how they made the zombies," Dusty remarked, as the invasion force gathered after searching the mission.* He glanced at Belle and Tragg, continuing, "So, happen you-all don't need us anymore, we'll head into town and grab some sleep before we go and fetch along our herd."

"Not *me!*" Waco put in, from where he was standing with Mark and the Kid.

"Why not?" Dusty asked, although he had a good idea of what was coming.

"Way I recollect it," the youngster replied, "you-all fired me and set me afoot in the Man on the Wall Saloon and I don't work for you no more. So, happen you've a mind to get back my invaluable services, you're going to have to come in there and offer most humble to take me on again."

"All right," the small Texan said, slapping the young blond on the back. "Although I'm damned if I know *what* invaluable services, I reckon you've earned *that.*"

* There had been only one fatal casualty among the hired guns, or their assailants, on the banks of the river. Silkie Roelich was shot and killed when he refused to surrender.—J.T.E.

APPENDIX ONE

During the War between the States, at seventeen years of age, Dustine Edward Marsden "Dusty" Fog had won promotion to captain in the field and was placed in command of the Texas Light Cavalry's hard-riding, harder-fighting Company C.[1] Leading them in the Arkansas campaign, he had earned the reputation of being an exceptionally capable military raider the equal of the South's other exponents, John Singleton Mosby and Turner Ashby.[2] In addition to preventing a pair of Union fanatics from starting an Indian uprising that would have decimated much of Texas,[3] he had supported Belle Boyd, the Rebel Spy, *q.v.*, on two very dangerous missions.[4]

When the war ended, he had become the *segundo* of the great OD Connected ranch in Rio Hondo County, Texas. Its owner and his uncle, General Jackson Baines "Ole Devil" Hardin,[5] had been crippled in a riding accident[6] and it had thrown much of the work—including handling an assignment with the future good relations between the United

1. Told in You're in Command Now, Mr. Fog.
2. Told in The Big Gun; Under the Stars and Bars; The Fastest Gun in Texas, and Kill Dusty Fog.
3. Told in The Devil Gun.
4. See Appendix Five.
5. Details of General Jackson Baines Hardin's early career are given in the "Ole Devil" series. His sobriquet came about because in those days he had deliberately sought to enhance the Mephistophelian aspect of his face and because his contemporaries had claimed he was a "li'l ole devil for a fight."
6. Told in the "The Paint" episode of The Fastest Gun in Texas.

States and Mexico at stake[7]—upon him. After having been sent to gather horses for the ranch's depleted remuda,[8] he acted as Colonel Charles Goodnight's *segundo* on the trail drive to Fort Sumner, New Mexico, which had done much to help Texas recover from the impoverished state in which the war had left its population.[9] With that achieved he had been equally successful in helping Goodnight to prove it would be possible to take herds of cattle to the railroad in Kansas.[10]

Having proven himself to be a first-class cavalry officer and cowhand, Dusty went on to gain acclaim as a trail boss,[11] roundup captain,[12] town-taming lawman,[13] and in later years, after his marriage to Lady Winifred Amelia Besgrove-Woodstole,[14] a diplomat. In a competition at the Cochise County Fair, in Arizona, he won the title of the Fastest Gun in the West, by beating many other exponents of the *pistolero* arts.[15]

Dusty Fog never found his lack of stature a disadvantage. In addition to being exceptionally strong he had taught himself to be completely ambidextrous. Possessing lightning-fast reflexes, he could draw and fire either or both of his Colts with great speed and accuracy. General Hardin's valet, Tommy Okasi,[16] was a trained Japanese samurai warrior

7. Told in THE YSABEL KID.
8. Told in .44 CALIBER MAN and A HORSE CALLED MOGOLLON.
9. Told in GOODNIGHT'S DREAM (American title, THE FLOATING OUTFIT) and FROM HIDE AND HORN.
10. Told in SET TEXAS BACK ON HER FEET and THE HIDE AND TALLOW MEN.
11. Told in TRAIL BOSS.
12. Told in THE MAN FROM TEXAS.
13. Told in QUIET TOWN; THE MAKING OF A LAWMAN; THE TROUBLE BUSTERS; THE SMALL TEXAN, and THE TOWN TAMERS.
14. Their grandson, Alvin Dustine "Cap" Fog, was the best combat pistol shot of his generation and the youngest man ever to become a captain in the Texas Rangers. See: "CAP" FOG, TEXAS RANGER, MEET MR. J. G. REEDER.
15. Told in GUN WIZARD.
16. "Tommy Okasi" is an Americanized corruption of the name he gave when picked up from a derelict vessel in the China Sea by a ship under the command of General Hardin's father. The author is unable to state why a trained samurai was compelled to flee from his homeland. The various members of the Hardin, Fog, and Blaze clan with whom we discussed the

and from him, Dusty learned jujitsu and karate. Although the arrival of Commodore Perry's flotilla of United States Navy warships in 1853–54 had brought increased contact with Japan, its martial arts had not yet received much publicity in the Western Hemisphere. So the knowledge was very useful when Dusty had to fight with bare hands against larger and heavier men.

---

matter in Fort Worth, Texas, in 1975 said that, because of the circumstances and the high social standing of the people involved—all of whom have descendants holding positions of importance and influence in Japan at the time of writing—it is inadvisable even at this late date to make the facts public. Details of how Tommy made use of his samurai training are given in the "Ole Devil" series.

APPENDIX TWO

With his exceptional good looks and magnificent physical development, Mark Counter presented the kind of appearance many people expected of Dusty Fog *q.v.*, and they took advantage of this when the need arose.[1]

When serving as a lieutenant in the Confederate cavalry, Mark's merits as an efficient and capable officer had been overshadowed by his taste in uniforms. Always a dandy dresser, coming from a wealthy family had enabled him to indulge in his whims, and as in later years he tended to help set the fashion for cowhand attire, his style of clothing was much copied.[2]

At the end of the War between the States, Mark had accompanied General Bushrod Sheldon's command into Mexico to fight for Emperor Maximilian. There he had helped Dusty Fog and the Ysabel Kid, *q.v.*, to accomplish the former's mission.[3] On returning to Texas he had been invited to join the OD Connected's floating outfit.[4] Knowing that his elder brothers and father, Big Rance Counter, could run the

1. One example is given in THE SOUTH WILL RISE AGAIN.
2. See the various volumes of the "Civil War" Series.
3. See seventh footnote, APPENDIX ONE.
4. Floating outfit: a group of four to six cowhands employed on a large ranch to work the more distant sections of the property. Taking food in a chuck wagon, or "greasy sack" on the back of a mule, they would be away from a ranch house for days at a time. Because of General Hardin's prominence in the affairs of Texas, the OD Connected's floating outfit were frequently sent to assist his friends who found themselves in difficulties or danger.

R over C ranch in the Big Bend country without his help and feeling that life would be more exciting with Dusty and the Kid, he had accepted.

An expert cowhand, Mark was known as Dusty's right bower[5] and gained acclaim by virtue of his enormous strength and ability in a roughhouse brawl. However, spending so much time in the small Texan's company, his full potential as a gunfighter received little attention. Men who were in a position to know claimed that he was second only to Dusty in the matter of speed and accuracy.

Many women found Mark irresistible, including Martha "Calamity Jane" Canary.[6] Only one of them held his heart, the lady outlaw Belle Starr.[7] It was several years after her death that he courted and married Dawn Sutherland, whom he had met on Colonel Charles Goodnight's trail drive to Fort Sumner, *q.v.*[8]

---

5. Right bower: second highest trump card in the game of euchre.

6. Mark's main meetings with Calamity Jane are told in TROUBLED RANGE; THE WILDCATS, and THE FORTUNE HUNTERS. He also makes a "guest appearance" in THE BIG HUNT of the "Calamity Jane" series.

7. How Mark's romance with Belle Starr commenced, progressed, and ended is told in the "The Bounty on Belle Starr's Scalp" episode of TROUBLED RANGE; RANGELAND HERCULES; the "The Lady Known as Belle" episode of THE HARD RIDERS and GUNS IN THE NIGHT. She also appears in HELL IN THE PALO DURO and GO BACK TO HELL, assisting Dusty Fog and Ysabel Kid.

8. Two of Mark's great-grandchildren achieved considerable fame on their own behalf. Details of Deputy Sheriff Bradford Counter's career are given in the "Rockabye County" series covering modern jet-age Texas law enforcement and James Allenvale Gunn, some of whom's career is described in the "Bunduki" series.

APPENDIX THREE

The only daughter of Long Walker, war leader of the Pehnane—Wasp, Quick Stinger, or Raider—Comanche Dog Soldier lodge and his French Creole *pairaivo*[1] married an Irish Kentuckian adventurer called Sam Ysabel, but died giving birth to their first child. Given the name Loncey Dalton, the boy was raised in the fashion of the Nemenuh.[2] With his father away much of the time on the family's businesses of mustanging and smuggling, his education had been left to his maternal grandfather.[3] From Long Walker he had learned those things which a Comanche warrior needed to know; how to ride the wildest freshly caught mustang, or when raiding—a polite name for the favorite Nemenuh pastime of stealing horses—to subjugate any domesticated mount to his will; to follow the faintest of tracks and conceal signs of his own passing; to locate hidden enemies, yet remain concealed himself if this was demanded by the situation; to move in silence even on the darkest of nights and to be proficient with a variety of weapons. In all these subjects he had proved an excellent pupil. He had inherited his father's rifle-shooting expertise, as was proved when he won the magnificent "One of a Thousand" Winchester Model of 1873 rifle that was offered as marksmanship prize at the

1. *Pairaivo:* first, or favorite, wife.
2. Nemenuh: "The People," the Comanche Indians' name for their nation.
3. Told in COMANCHE.

Cochise County Fair.[4] While he was not really fast with his Colt Second Model Dragoon revolver, he could perform adequately when needed. However, his best weapon, the use of which gained him his Nemenuh man-name Cuchilo, was the James Black bowie knife. It was claimed that he could equal the designer of the knife,[5] Colonel James Bowie,[6] in wielding the massive and deadly blade.[7]

Joining his father on smuggling trips along the Rio Grande, having heard him referred to as Sam Ysabel's Kid, the Mexicans called him "Cabrito." Smuggling did not attract mild-mannered pacifists, but even the toughest and roughest men on the bloody border between Texas and Mexico learned that it did not pay to antagonize Sam Ysabel's son. His education and upbringing had not been such that he was possessed of an overinflated sense of the sanctity of human life. When crossed, he dealt with the situation like a Pehnane Dog Soldier—being a member of that lodge—swiftly and in a deadly effective manner.

During the War between the States, after serving as scouts for the "Gray Ghost," Colonel John Singleton Mosby, *q.v.*, the Kid and his father were sent to utilize their specialized knowledge by collecting and delivering to the Confederate authorities in Texas supplies that had been run through the U.S. Navy's blockade into the Mexican port of Matamoros. It had been hard and dangerous work, but never more so than

4. Told in GUN WIZARD.

5. Some researchers claim that the actual designer of the knife was James Bowie's eldest brother, Rezin Pleasant.

6. What happened to James Bowie's knife after his death in the final assault on the Alamo Mission, San Antonio de Bexar, on 6th March, 1836, is told in GET URREA and THE QUEST FOR BOWIE'S BLADE.

7. As all of James Black's bowie knives were handmade, there was a slight variation in their dimensions. That in the Kid's possession had a blade two and a half inches wide, eleven and a half inches long, and a quarter of an inch thick. Bowie's knife weighed forty-three ounces, having its blade eleven inches long, two and a quarter inches wide, and three eighths of an inch thick. One thing they all had in common was a clip point, where the last few inches of the back of the blade joins the main cutting edge in a concave arc and is sharpened to form an extension of it.

on the two occasions when they had been involved in missions with Belle Boyd, *q.v.*[8]

Sam Ysabel had been murdered soon after the end of the war. While hunting his killers the Kid had met first Dusty Fog and then Mark Counter.[9] Ending the mission successfully and learning that the Kid no longer intended to go on smuggling, Dusty had offered him employment on the OD Connected. Pointing out that he knew little about the work of a cowhand, he was told that it was his skill as a scout that would be required.

The Kid's presence as a member of Ole Devil Hardin's floating outfit had been of great benefit all around. Dusty had gained another loyal friend who was ready to stick by him in any danger. The ranch acquired the services of a capable and efficient scout. For his part the Kid was turned from a life of petty crime that could easily have developed into more serious breaking of the law and became a useful member of society. Peace officers and law-abiding citizens might have been thankful for that, as he would have made a deadly and murderous outlaw if he had been driven to such a life. It had been in a major part due to his efforts that most of the Comanche Indian bands agreed to go on to the reservation.[10] Nor could Dusty have cleaned out the outlaw town of Hell without his assistance.[11]

8. See APPENDIX FIVE.
9. See seventh footnote, APPENDIX ONE.
10. Told in SIDEWINDER.
11. Told in HELL IN THE PALO DURO and GO BACK TO HELL.

APPENDIX FOUR

Left an orphan almost from birth by a Waco Indian raid, from whence had come the only name he knew, Waco had been raised as part of a North Texas rancher's large family.[1] Guns had always been a part of his life, and his sixteenth birthday had seen him riding with Clay Allison's tough, hardbitten "wild onion" crew. The CA hands, like their employer, were notorious for their wild ways and frequently dangerous behavior. Living in the company of such men, all older than himself, he had grown quick to take offense and eager to defend himself with his lightning-fast draw and accurate shooting skill. It had seemed to be only a matter of time before one shootout too many would have seen him branded as a killer and fleeing from the law with a price on his head.

Fortunately for Waco that day did not come. From the moment that Dusty Fog, *q.v.*, saved his life—at considerable risk to his own—the youngster had started to change for the better.[2] Leaving Allison, with the Washita curly wolf's blessing, he had become a member of Ole Devil Hardin's floating outfit. From the other members of this elite brotherhood, who treated him as a favorite younger sibling, he had learned many useful lessons. The Ysabel Kid taught him to read tracks and act as a scout. Mark Counter, *q.v.*, gave him instruction in barehanded self-defense. A gambler of their

---

1. How Waco repaid his debt to his adoptive father is told in WACO'S DEBT.
2. Told in TRIGGER FAST.

acquaintance, Frank Derringer, instructed him in the ways of crooked and honest gamblers.[3] From Dusty Fog he learned much that would help him to gain fame as a peace officer of exceptional merit.[4] What was more, although he already knew *how* to shoot, he had learned when it was mandatory for him to do so.

From his education at his friends' hands Waco was to become in later years a respected and extremely competent peace officer. He served with distinction in the Arizona Rangers,[5] as sheriff of Two Forks County, Utah,[6] and finally as a U.S. marshal.[7]

3. Told in THE MAKING OF A LAWMAN and THE TROUBLE BUSTERS.
4. Early examples of Waco's ability as a peace officer are given in the "The Hired Butcher" episode of THE HARD RIDERS and the "A Tolerable Straight Shooting Gun" episode of THE FLOATING OUTFIT (British title).
5. Told in SAGEBRUSH SLEUTH, ARIZONA RANGER, and WACO RIDES IN.
6. Told in THE DRIFTER and, by inference, in DOC LEROY, M.D.
7. Told in HOUND DOG MAN.

APPENDIX FIVE

Wanting a son and learning that his wife, Electra, could not have any more children, Vincent Charles Boyd had insisted upon giving his only daughter, Belle,[1] thorough training in several subjects not normally regarded as being a necessary part of a wealthy southron girl's education. At seventeen she could ride a horse—astride or sidesaddle—as well as any of her male neighbors, men who were to help supply the Confederate States with its superlative cavalry. In addition she was a skilled performer with an *épée de combat*,[2] an excellent shot with a pistol or rifle, and expert at savate, French foot and fist boxing. All of which were to stand her in good stead.

Shortly before the commencement of the War between the States, a mob of pro-Union rabble had stormed the Boyd plantation. Before they were driven off by the family's Negro servants, they had murdered her parents and set fire to her home. Belle was wounded in the fighting and, on recovering, joined her cousin, Rose Greenhow,[3] who was operating a spy ring. Wanting to find the two leaders of the mob, Belle had not been content to remain in one place. Instead, she

1. According to the researches of American fictionist genealogist Philip José Farmer, Belle Boyd is the grand-aunt of Jane Porter, who married the seventh Lord Greystoke, whose biography is given in the Tarzan of the Apes series of books by Edgar Rice Burroughs.

2. An *épée de combat* is basically a thrusting weapon, although it also has a cutting edge.

3. Some details of Rose Greenhow's career are given in Kill Dusty Fog!

had taken the more dangerous task of delivering the other agents' information to the Confederate authorities. Gaining proficiency and earning the nickname the "Rebel Spy," she had graduated to handling more important and risky assignments. On two of them she had worked with Dusty Fog, *q.v.*,[4] and a third brought her into contact with the Ysabel Kid.[5] However, she had not brought her quest for the murderers of her parents to a successful conclusion until shortly after the end of the war.[6]

While the Yankees might have had every reason to hate the Rebel Spy during the war, she had given them no cause to feel other than gratitude to her once it was over. On signing the oath of allegiance to the Union she had been allowed to join the United States Secret Service. Despite the trouble she had given to that organization throughout the hostilities, she had served it loyally and with efficiency. Assisted by the lady outlaw Belle Starr, *q.v.*, and Martha "Calamity Jane" Canary,[7] she had brought an end to the reign of terror created by the murderous "Bad Bunch."[8] Then she had broken up the Brotherhood for Southern Freedom, with the aid of Ole Devil Hardin's floating outfit, *q.v.*[9] Her participation in thwarting an attempt to murder President U. S. Grant had prevented trouble between the northern and southern states.[10] Later, she was involved in Octavius Xavier Guillemot's attempt to gain possession of James Bowie's knife.[11] Then she called upon Calamity Jane once more to help in averting what might have developed into a war between the United States and Great Britain.

4. Told in The Colt and the Saber and The Rebel Spy.
5. Told in The Bloody Border.
6. Told in Back to the Bloody Border.
7. Details of Martha Jane Canary's career are given in the author's "Calamity Jane" series.
8. Told in The Bad Bunch.
9. Told in To Arms, To Arms, in Dixie! and The South Will Rise Again.
10. Told in The Hooded Riders.
11. Told in The Whip and the War Lance.